THE TOWER BRIDGE MURDER

An Augusta Peel Mystery Book 4

EMILY ORGAN

The Augusta Peel Series

Chapter 1

A JANUARY SLEET was falling as Mary Willis stepped out of Fenchurch Street railway station. After the heavy rain of the previous evening, it had grown colder overnight. The icy flakes melted as they landed on the wet ground. People hurried past with umbrellas, while others dashed into waiting taxis. Mary paused, looking around to get her bearings. She was in Railway Place and the shops were opening for the day. Shutters were being lifted and awnings pulled down to protect customers from the weather.

Mary wanted to travel by taxi, but she had to choose the cheaper option of taking the bus. The cloakroom attendant had told her to take the number twenty-five from Leadenhall Street and get off at High Holborn. Mary worked out the direction she needed and began walking, swapping the suitcase from one hand to the other when its weight became too much.

The bus took a while to arrive and was filled with the odour of damp clothing. It trundled along Cheapside and Mary glimpsed St Paul's Cathedral through the misty windows before the bus turned into Newgate Street.

She disembarked in High Holborn where everyone was in a hurry to get out of the sleet. Everyone except a bent old lady who stood on the corner selling sprigs of lucky heather for a sixpence. Mary ignored her as she lugged her suitcase towards Southampton Row.

'Mary Willis?' said Mrs Flynn, the landlady of the lodging house. 'You're earlier than I expected.'

'I caught an earlier train.'

'So you did.' She spoke with an Irish accent and had dark greying hair and a freckled complexion. 'Where've you travelled from?'

'Bournemouth.'

'Well, you did get going early. Luckily your room's already available. I'll show you to it.'

The room was in the attic and simply furnished with a small bed, wardrobe and washstand. A little window overlooked the noisy street.

'And you're staying for a week?'

'To begin with. Can I stay longer if need be?'

'Yes, that will be fine. You need to pay me upfront, though. One pound.'

Mary had the money for now, but she needed to find work. She took the money from her purse and handed it to Mrs Flynn.

'Thank you. Breakfast is served at half-past seven and tea at half-past six. Don't be late for either, else you'll miss out.'

'I need to find work. Do you know of anywhere?'

'What sort of thing are you looking for?'

'I've worked in a cafe before. I could do that.'

'Well my sister runs a shop close by. She's looking for someone and you might do. Do you have a reference?'

Mary nodded.

'Let me see it.' Mrs Flynn held out her hand.

Mary opened her suitcase, pulled out an envelope from its inner pocket, and handed it to the landlady. Mrs Flynn ran her eyes over it before handing it back.

'I'll telephone her,' she said. 'And if she likes the sound of you, then she'll probably want to see you first thing tomorrow. I'll let you know.'

'Thank you.'

It was a promising start.

Chapter 2

'IT'S DEFINITELY COLDER OUT THERE today,' said Augusta Peel, turning the sign on her Bloomsbury shop door to "open". 'I hope the weather doesn't keep the customers away.'

'Hopefully it won't,' said her assistant, Fred. He was a dark-skinned young man who wore spectacles and a tweed suit. 'With a bit of luck, they'll come in here to keep warm.'

'Let's hope so.' Fortunately, the bookshop was heated by an efficient stove and, with walls of second-hand books and chairs to read them in, the place felt cosy.

Less cosy was Augusta's draughty workshop at the back of the shop. It was an improvement on the basement she had previously worked in, but she had to wear a lot of layers while in there repairing books.

'The Tower Bridge mystery,' said Fred, who was reading a newspaper at the counter.

'The what?'

'Haven't you read about it yet?'

'Not yet. What happened?' She walked over to peer at the story over his shoulder.

'A bloodstained bag was found on Tower Bridge last night at about eight o'clock.'

'Bloodstained?'

'Not nice, is it? There was nothing valuable inside it but a library card was found which was in the name of Celia Hawkins.'

'So something's happened to Celia Hawkins?'

'It seems so. The police have issued a description of her. She's twenty-four with brown eyes and fair hair and is five feet and four inches tall. She works in a clothes store in Battersea.'

'I hope she's alright. Hopefully, they'll find her soon enough.'

'I hope so, too. It sounds like someone robbed her, took the valuables and discarded the bag. But the fact it was bloodstained doesn't sound good. And why would she have gone missing?'

'I can see why it's being described as a mystery. Are there any more details?'

'No, that's it. There was presumably little time to include more as it must have been close to the deadline for printing last night.'

Augusta wondered what Detective Inspector Philip Fisher made of it. She hadn't seen him since they had worked together on the Bloomsbury murders the previous autumn. Perhaps this new mystery would prompt him to call on her.

She opened the bag of bird seed she kept behind the counter and fed some to Sparky, the canary who perched in his cage on the counter. Sparky belonged to her friend Lady Hereford, but Augusta had been looking after him for the past few months. Her caring duties had begun when Lady Hereford was being treated in hospital and, although she was now living at the nearby Russell Hotel, she felt Sparky was happier with Augusta. He seemed to enjoy watching the customers in the shop and, if they were lucky, he'd treat them to a little song.

'I suppose I'd better get on with repairing that copy of *Howard's End*,' said Augusta, picking up her fingerless gloves.

'Shall I make you a cup of tea to warm you up in there?'

'That would be lovely. Thank you, Fred.'

Howard's End had been poorly treated by someone in the past. The spine was broken, coffee had been spilt over the cover and countless pages had their corners turned down. Sometimes it was difficult to decide whether to repair a book or dispose of it. But this copy was a first edition from 1910, so Augusta wanted to do the best she could with it.

She tucked her auburn hair behind her ears and set to work on cleaning the cover. She thought about Celia Hawkins as she worked. If the incident had been a straightforward robbery, then why was Celia missing? And the weather the previous evening had been atrocious - pouring rain and a strong wind. There couldn't have been many people on Tower Bridge at that time.

Fred appeared in the doorway with her cup of tea. 'Mr Fairburn is here to see you,' he said, wrinkling his nose with distaste.

'Mr Fairburn from Webster's bookshop around the corner?'

'Yes.'

'The bookshop you used to work in, but he dismissed you when he took it over?'

'Yes.'

'Did he say what he wants?'

'No.'

'Interesting.' Augusta took the cup from him and enjoyed the warmth against her gloved palms. 'I suppose I'd better see him then.'

Mr Fairburn was a bald man with a thick moustache and spectacles. He looked about fifty - ten years older than Augusta. He wore a smart pinstriped suit and had the appearance of a bank manager rather than a bookseller.

'Mrs Peel, I presume?'

'Yes. Mr Fairburn, I believe?'

'That's correct. I didn't realise Fred now works in your shop.'

'Did you not? He's been working here for about two months now.'

'You do realise he used to work in my shop?'

'Yes. And he gave me your name as a reference. I never followed up on it, I could tell he would be good at his job.' She gave Fred a smile. 'He told me that when you took over from Mr Webster, you brought along your own staff, and he was no longer required.'

'A regrettable decision, but I had to maintain my loyalty to my existing staff. It's a little perturbing to discover a former employee is now working for a competitor close by.'

'I think Fred made a sensible choice. He enjoyed working in Webster's and when that job came to an end, he then chose another bookshop close by. Anyone in his position would have done the same. May I ask what you wish to speak to me about, Mr Fairburn?'

'Before you occupied these premises, Mrs Peel, this shop was a magic shop.'

'That's right. Run by Mr H W Matravers. He had to retire because of ill health and went to live with his daughter and her husband.'

'I believe so. This place wasn't a bookshop then.'

'You're right, it wasn't.' Augusta sipped her tea. She was already growing tired of Mr Fairburn. He had a pedantic manner about him and she didn't like the way he kept sniffing and darting his eyes around.

'When this was a magic shop, everything was going swimmingly,' he said.

'I'm pleased to hear it.'

'Now that it's a bookshop, however, business is not going quite so well.'

'Is it not?'

'To save your time this morning, Mrs Peel, I'll put this in the bluntest of terms. You're stealing customers from me.'

'Am I? I'm sorry to hear it. It's not something I set out to do.'

'What you set out to do is irrelevant. The fact is, you're having a detrimental effect on my business. There are simply not enough customers in this locality for two book-shops to coexist in such close proximity to each other. Webster's has enjoyed its location here for over forty years. Your shop has been here for how long? Two, three months? It stands to reason that the most recently estab-lished business should be the one which moves elsewhere.'

Augusta choked on a mouthful of tea. 'You're asking me to move my shop, Mr Fairburn?'

'In simple terms, yes.'

'What a preposterous suggestion!'

'Not really. Put yourself in my shoes, Mrs Peel.' She glanced down at them and noticed they were very shiny. 'Imagine you've invested a lot of time and money in a long-established bookshop, then discover you're losing customers to a tawdry new establishment which has just opened its doors around the corner. And a shop which has a budgerigar in it too! That can't be hygienic.'

'He's a canary, and he's more hygienic than most people I know. If I were in your shoes, Mr Fairburn, then I would ask myself why I was losing customers to a new business. I might wonder if the new establishment had a better offering than my own.'

'I find that an impertinent response.'

'And I call it common sense. If you're losing customers, then you're probably not giving them what they want. At no point have I ever set out to steal business from you. I'm merely selling the books which I repair. This seems to be popular with my customers because they like the character of an old book, and they can buy it for a cheaper price than a new one.'

'And there lies the problem! You're deliberately under-cutting my prices. You're luring my customers away!'

'Perhaps you could also sell second-hand books, Mr Fairburn?'

'I have no room on my shelves to do so, and nor do I wish to.'

'I suspect we attract different types of customers,' said Augusta. 'There's the type who likes a nice new book and will pay a good price for it. I would say that's the sort of customer who would visit your shop. There's another type of customer who likes second-hand books and doesn't have as much money to spend. I suspect they also like canaries and friendly shop assistants like Fred. Those are the people who come to my bookshop, Mr Fairburn. I can't imagine many of them liking yours.'

Mr Fairburn's moustache bristled. 'I can see I'm not getting through to you, Mrs Peel. I have to get back to my shop now, but this matter is far from resolved. You're clearly a stubborn individual with very fixed ideas. I hope I won't have to engage my lawyers on this.'

Augusta couldn't resist a laugh. 'Lawyers?'

'You wait and see, Mrs Peel.' He pointed a finger at her. 'Just you wait and see.'

Chapter 3

THE LANDLADY'S SISTER, Mrs Saunders, was interested in taking Mary on. So the following morning, she walked the short distance to Grenville Street, a little street of shops and respectable houses, a short walk from Brunswick Square. Mary wasn't familiar with Bloomsbury and she decided she liked the rows of neat Georgian houses and tree-filled squares. She had grown up accustomed to shabbier surroundings.

Saunders Animal Supplies advertised dog food, chicken food and food for caged birds. As well as animal feed, it sold seeds and bulbs. Sacks of corn were arranged in the window.

Inside, the counter ran along three walls of the shop and the shelves were stacked to the ceiling. A young woman stood on a ladder, retrieving a box of something for a man with a Jack Russell dog at his heel. The shop smelt of grain and malt. Mary quite liked it. She waited for the woman to finish serving the man, then asked to speak to Mrs Saunders.

'What name shall I give?' The young woman had

bobbed hair and fashionable pencil-thin eyebrows. She wore a grubby canvas apron over a stylish lavender dress. Mary wondered if she would prefer to be working somewhere more glamorous.

'Mary Willis.'

The woman disappeared through a door behind the counter and, a short while later, a lady in a khaki work coat appeared. She had short-cropped hair and spoke with an Irish accent like her sister. 'My sister has told me all about you. I hear you have a good reference.'

'Yes. Would you like to see it?'

'No, it's fine, she's already told me all about it and I trust her. A cafe in Bournemouth, I hear?'

'That's right.'

'My late husband had an aunt in Bournemouth.'

'Really?'

'She may well have been a customer of yours.' She smiled, and Mary hoped this was a good sign. 'My sister can be quite particular about who she has staying with her so, with that in mind, and the good reference, I suggest a week's trial starting tomorrow.'

Mary grinned. 'That's wonderful news, thank you.'

'What do you know about animal feed?'

'Nothing, I'm afraid. But I can learn fast.'

'Lucy here is happy to show you the ropes.'

Lucy didn't seem happy to do so. Mary gave her a smile, which wasn't returned.

'Wages are one pound, six shillings per week. We'll see you here at eight o'clock tomorrow,' said Mrs Saunders.

Mary left the shop with a skip in her step. She had somewhere to stay, and she had a job.

She stopped off at a Lyon's Cornerhouse and treated herself to a cup of coffee to celebrate.

'Normal.' He wasn't going to tell the detective what had passed between them. It was none of his business.

'And when did you realise she was missing from home?'

'I got back at nine that night and she weren't there.'

'Did Miss Hawkins tell you what she planned to do that day?'

'She didn't tell me, but I knew she was going to work like she always did.'

'And she worked at…' The detective consulted his notes again. 'Furnival Fashions clothes shop on Lavender Hill.'

'Yeah. And I know she went to the shop that day because I went in there the next day looking for her. They told me she'd been in the day before, but she hadn't turned up that morning. Then someone told me her bag was found on the bridge. You know all this, anyway. Speaking to me isn't going to help find the murderer.'

'Trust us to do our job, Mr Barnes. Where did you get your black eye from?'

'A fight.'

'With who?'

'I'm not saying.'

'You're not helping yourself by withholding information from us, Mr Barnes. Now, do you know what Celia was doing on Tower Bridge?'

'No, I had no idea she was going there.'

'Can you think of any reason for her to be there?'

'The only reason she'd go near there was to visit St John Horsleydown church in Bermondsey, where her parents got married. She went there each year on the anniversary of her mother's death. Her mother's buried out at Brookwood but Celia preferred to visit St John's because her mother grew up round there. She got buried out in Surrey when she had nothing to do with the place.'

'Like many Londoners,' said Detective Inspector Petty. 'The graveyards in this city filled up a long time ago. When was the anniversary of her mother's death?'

'Middle of December some time. So Celia went there then. That's when she got robbed.'

'Robbed? What happened?'

'She'd visited the church in Bermondsey and she was crossing the bridge to visit me in Old Jewry police station because the City police were holding me there for something I didn't do. She was walking across the bridge when some girl, woman... I don't know which, robbed her. She had a knife, and she took Celia's bag.'

'Presumably Miss Hawkins reported it to the police?'

'Yeah, but you lot did nothing about it. You're more interested in harassing people like me.'

'Could that be because you're a career criminal, Mr Barnes?' said Sergeant Gosling. He had sharp features and neat grey whiskers.

'Don't know what you're talking about. And it's not relevant, we're talking about what happened to Celia. I don't know why she went to Tower Bridge the other night. She never mentioned to me she was going there.'

'Tower Bridge is over five miles from where Miss Hawkins lived and worked,' said Detective Inspector Petty.

'I know. Like I say, I don't know what she was doing there.'

'And she didn't need to cross the bridge to get to the church because it's on this side of the river,' said the sergeant. 'She must have been heading for somewhere on the north side. Any idea where?'

'No.' Tommy didn't like the way both policemen stared at him, scrutinising his face for any hint of deceit.

'Is it possible she arranged to meet someone?' asked the detective inspector.

'She could've done. But I would've thought she'd have told me about it.'

'Did she often meet friends without telling you?'

'No.'

'Did she usually return home after work or did she often go elsewhere?'

'She usually came home. I never knew her to go off like that before without telling me.'

'So it was unusual?'

'Yeah. All of it's unusual!' He felt a snap of impatience. He was tired of the boring questions. 'You need to be out there looking for the killer! There's nothing I can tell you that's going to help with finding them!'

'You say you got home at nine o'clock that evening,' said Detective Inspector Petty. 'And to clarify, this was Monday the tenth of January. What were you doing before you got home?'

'Working.'

'Where?'

'In Clapham. Helping a friend move some stuff.'

'What sort of stuff?'

Tommy felt his jaw clench. Why was this relevant?

'Just some goods which he sells at the market.'

'Who is this friend?'

'He won't want me giving you his name.'

'I'm sure he won't. But we need his name so he can provide an alibi for you.'

Tommy sighed and tried to calm his anger by running a hand through his hair. 'I don't need an alibi. I've done nothing wrong!'

Chapter 5

Sir Charles Granger settled into his usual chair at the Drummond Club, rested his gold-topped cane against the seat, ordered a whisky from the waiter, and lit a cigar. The club lounge was furnished in sage green, lit with subdued lighting, and had comfortable leather chairs which were shiny and cracked with age. Portraits of important men and glamorous women hung on the walls. Sir Charles had a soft spot for the Duchess of Sedgby, a blonde beauty in a blue dress who gazed adoringly at him from her picture above the fireplace.

A waiter brought Sir Charles his drink as he opened his book, *The Moonstone* by Wilkie Collins. He had only a few chapters left to read. Who took the diamond? He couldn't wait to find out. He read three pages before he was disturbed.

'Charlie!' An old friend approached.

'Hello, Piggers.' It was a name he had used for Sir Gregory Pole-Mateland since their schoolboy days at Eton. Piggers was a stocky man with grey curly hair, little round eyes and red cheeks.

He sank into a neighbouring chair and dropped a newspaper onto the table. Sir Charles eyed it and gave a sneer. 'What are you doing reading that rag?'

Piggers laughed. 'You're annoyed it's not one of your papers?'

'Exactly.'

'The Drummond Club is obliged to furnish us with all the daily newspapers.'

'But it doesn't mean you should read them.'

'Come now, Charlie. You know my loyalties lie with you. In fact, I've just been reading something quite interesting, actually.' He picked up the paper and leafed through it. 'Here we are. There's an article about that poor girl who was murdered on Tower Bridge and thrown into the Thames. They've printed a photograph of her. I'd say she looks familiar, wouldn't you?'

Sir Charles sighed. He didn't want to hear about it. He took a sip of his drink and watched Piggers hold up the newspaper so he could see the picture of Celia Hawkins.

It was a studio portrait, taken fairly recently. Celia's hair was fair and shiny, and she was fine featured with a prominent nose. The nose was a flaw which meant she wasn't beautiful in a conventional sense, but Sir Charles was drawn to little imperfections.

'Who is she?' he asked, attempting to sound as disinterested as possible.

'Miss Celia Hawkins. You heard about the murder, didn't you?'

'I did.'

'Dreadful! They've interviewed her common-law husband.'

'Have they?'

'It says here that Tommy Barnes, a thirty-three-year-old man from Battersea, has been spoken to. I expect he must have done it.'

'It sounds like the case is solved then.'

'But if it was him, then why would he commit the crime on Tower Bridge, of all places? That's uncommon, that is.'

'Who knows what goes through the mind of a maniac like that. Why don't you order yourself a drink, Piggers?' He returned to his book.

'I will. There's something else which strikes me as uncommon about this.'

'What's that?'

'I think I've seen this Celia Hawkins before.'

'You have?'

'Yes. She looks just like the lady I saw you dining with at L'Épicurien restaurant in Covent Garden a few weeks ago. Don't you think?' Piggers held up the paper again to show him. Sir Charles raised his eyes with as much disinterest as possible, then looked back at his book.

'Looks nothing like her.'

'Oh come on. I think she does!'

Sir Charles did his best to ignore the ball of irritation which was now building in his chest. 'The thing is, Piggers, these days women in their twenties all look the same. Don't you find? They all insist on their hair cut a certain way and they all wear the same rouge and lipstick. They all wear the same clothes too. It's quite easy to mistake one for another.'

Piggers laughed. 'You're right there, Charlie. Who was the girl you were with when I saw you, then?'

'I can't remember. Georgina or something like that.'

'Pretty name. Waiter!'

Piggers ordered a drink and Sir Charles slowly exhaled.

The trouble with Piggers was he was smarter than he looked. Fortunately, on this occasion, Sir Charles had persuaded him he was mistaken. He had to watch him, though. If the murder received much more coverage, then questions would be asked again.

Chapter 6

AUGUSTA PUT the newly repaired copy of *Howard's End* on the shelf, next to *A Room with a View*. 'It's almost like new,' she said to Fred. 'If you're able to ignore the turned down page corners. Why do people do that? Why not use a bookmark?'

'Not everyone's got one.'

'But you can use anything as a bookmark. A strip of newspaper, a piece of string even. There's no need to vandalise the pages.'

'How much shall we sell it for?'

'It's a first edition, so I think a shilling would do.'

'I think we could charge more.'

'Do you think so?'

'One shilling and threepence.'

'Well, we could try it. Our customers might think that's too much though.'

'If they do, then we can reduce it.'

'We don't need to put our prices up though, just because Mr Fairburn complained.'

'No, I realise that. I'm just thinking about how we can

make a little more money. You put a lot of work into the repairs, Mrs Peel. You need to be paid well for it.'

'I don't suppose I can argue with that.'

The bell above the door rang as a nurse in a blue uniform opened it and wheeled in a large wicker bath chair. Fred dashed over to help.

In the bath chair sat Lady Hereford, and she was here for her weekly visit to see how Sparky was getting on.

Augusta thought her appearance had much improved since she had left hospital. Jewellery sparkled at her ears and throat. She wore a tweed cloche hat over her wavy white hair and her chocolate brown coat was trimmed with fur. Each cheek had a circle of rouge, and her lips were coloured fuchsia pink.

'Augusta! Fred! How are you both?'

'Very well, thank you, Lady Hereford,' said Augusta. 'Would you like tea?'

'Yes please.'

'I'll make the tea,' said Fred, and Augusta thanked him. The nurse pushed the chair over to the canary's cage. 'And how are you, Sparky?' asked Lady Hereford. 'Have you got a song for me? No, it doesn't look like it.'

Augusta fetched the bag of bird seed from behind the counter and handed it to Lady Hereford. The old lady opened the cage door and fed seeds to the little bird.

'Are you quite sure you don't want him to live with you in the Russell Hotel?' said Augusta.

'Quite sure. I don't think he'd like it there, he'd get very bored. He's a young canary about town and he likes it here in this shop where he can watch the comings and goings. I'm certain he would be completely fed up having to stare at my old face all day long.'

'I shouldn't think he'd mind at all,' said Augusta. 'But I'm happy to have him here with me for the time being.'

'Good, because he's such a bright little bird and likes to be kept entertained. I don't want him getting in your way though, Augusta. I know you're very busy. The murder on Tower Bridge is a terrible business, isn't it? I expect that dashing inspector will be calling on you soon to help him out.'

'Possibly, but I've not heard anything from him for several weeks.'

'Oh? Perhaps he's working somewhere else? I know the Scotland Yard chaps can get involved in cases all across the country.'

'Yes they can.' Augusta had assumed Philip would have informed her if he was going away somewhere. But maybe that had been a foolish assumption to make.

'So I suppose you're not involved at all with the case of the poor woman on Tower Bridge,' said Lady Hereford. 'I wonder if it was a robbery.'

'It might have been. An article in today's newspaper said she'd been robbed on Tower Bridge before.'

'How awful! And she went back again? What a strange thing to do. It sounds as though she was asking for trouble.'

'It wasn't her fault.'

'No, but if I'd been robbed on Tower Bridge, then I certainly wouldn't have returned there alone. And on a dark, rainy night! Quite strange if you ask me. It makes you wonder what Detective Inspector Fisher would make of it all. Let's hope he turns up soon. I like him. Why don't you telephone the Yard and find out where he is?'

'I don't think there's any need to.'

'But you've not heard from him for several weeks. Where's the man got to?'

'He's probably working somewhere else, as you've suggested.'

'But wouldn't you like to know for sure?'

'It's not really my business.'

'Well find out for me, then. I'm intrigued now! Have you got a telephone in this shop?'

'Yes.'

'Well, go on then. Telephone the Yard and ask for Detective Inspector Fisher.'

The telephone was on the wall behind the counter. Augusta stepped over to it and called the operator. She requested to be put through to Scotland Yard. Once through, she asked to speak to Philip.

'Detective Inspector Fisher is unavailable at the present time,' came the reply.

'May I ask where he is?'

'Who is this calling?'

'My name's Augusta Peel. I'm a friend of his.'

'I'm sure you can appreciate, madam, that anybody can telephone the Yard claiming to be a friend of one of our detective inspectors. We are not at liberty to disclose their whereabouts.'

'I see. Thank you for your time.' Augusta hung up the receiver.

Where was he?

The mystery perplexed her for the rest of the day. After she had closed the shop, she took Sparky to her flat, then took the bus to Westminster.

The imposing brick and granite buildings of New Scotland Yard overlooked the river. A chilly wind pulled at her hat and coat as she made her way through the tall gates.

Inside the wood-panelled reception area, a smart duty sergeant stood behind the desk.

'Is Detective Inspector Fisher here today?' she asked.

'I'll find out,' he replied. 'May I ask your name?'

'Mrs Augusta Peel.'

She waited for some time. Officious looking men came and went, all of them acknowledged her with a smile or a doff of their hat. But the longer she waited, the more despondent Augusta felt.

Eventually, the duty sergeant returned. 'I'm afraid Detective Inspector Fisher isn't here today.'

'Do you know when he will be?'

'I don't. Perhaps someone else can help you instead? What's your query regarding?'

'It's regarding him. I'm a friend of his. We were colleagues during the war, you see, and I haven't heard from him in a while. Do you know him?'

'I do, yes.'

'Have you seen him recently?'

'Not recently, but that's probably because I've been working on different shifts to him.'

'I find it odd I've not heard from him. Is there anyone else who can explain where he is or when he's likely to be here?'

'I'm afraid not. I can't provide any more information than I already have, Mrs Peel. Sorry about that.'

'He's definitely still employed by the Yard?'

'Oh yes. He hasn't left his position.'

She deduced the duty sergeant either knew nothing further or had been instructed to say nothing more. He went back behind the desk and began busying himself with some papers. There seemed little point in asking him more questions. There was a risk it would antagonise him.

After leaving Scotland Yard, Augusta crossed the road to the riverside wall. Heavy, grey clouds scurried across the sky and the breeze carried small flakes of sleet. Augusta collected her thoughts as she watched a barge passing beneath Westminster Bridge. On the opposite shore, barges were moored at the wharves in front of the warehouses and factories.

Augusta tried to reassure herself that all was well with Philip. From what she could glean from his colleagues, he was still working at the Yard, and they weren't concerned about him.

It didn't explain why she hadn't heard from him, though. Had she offended him in some way? She thought back to the investigation into the Bloomsbury murders and tried to recall each conversation they'd had. Then she checked herself, realising such analysis was probably uncalled for. Philip was probably working on a secret case, it was the only explanation she could think of.

She wondered which Scotland Yard detective was working on the Tower Bridge murder. It was the sort of case which appealed to Philip. It was also the sort of case they could have worked on well together. She wanted to learn more about what had happened that night and she wanted to discuss it with him.

Augusta turned and crossed the road again. She headed for Westminster tube station. A journey from there on the District Line would take her to Mark Lane station. And from there, it was only a short walk to Tower Bridge.

Chapter 7

'How old is the baby?' asked the detective, pointing at the infant Dora cuddled beneath her shawl.

'Two months,' she replied. Her baby son was sleeping, and she hoped the detective's officious voice wouldn't wake him. He had told her his name was Detective Inspector Petty, and he was from Scotland Yard. He was a large, red-haired man who seemed to take up most of the space in her little room. He was accompanied by Constable Farris, whom she recognised from Bermondsey police station. She watched the pair of them glance around the shabby room where she and her son lived, ate and slept. She sat on the only chair and there was a small bed in the corner. The room was cold, but she never lit the fire until after sundown to save money. As the two officers surveyed the room, Dora felt her face heat with shame. She knew they were passing judgement on her.

'Who do you live here with?' asked the detective inspector.

'My friends.'

'How many?'

'Three.'

'Can you give me their names?'

'They wouldn't want me to.'

'Where are they now?'

'They're out working.'

'Doing what?'

'Work.'

'I think I know what they'll be doing,' said the constable.

'What?' asked the detective inspector.

'Thieving.' He turned to Dora. 'Isn't that right, Miss Jones? You've done a bit of thieving in your time, haven't you?'

She chose not to answer. He was right, of course, but she wasn't going to humour him.

'I need to know who lives in this tenement flat,' said Detective Inspector Petty.

'I've forgotten,' said Dora.

'It's alright sir,' said the constable. 'I can give you their names. I've arrested them all enough times.'

'Very well.' The detective inspector addressed Dora again. 'Can you tell me where you were on the evening of Monday, the tenth of January?'

'Not on Tower Bridge murdering that woman, if that's what you're wondering.'

'Where were you then?'

'Here.'

'Can anyone vouch for that?'

'My friends. I wasn't on the bridge that night. I wouldn't have taken my baby out in the cold and rain. I'm not that stupid.'

He made some notes and Constable Farris spoke. 'Can you recall the last time we met, Miss Jones?'

'Yeah. You arrested me for stealing on Gainsford Street.'

'Is that right?' asked the detective inspector. The constable responded with a smug smile.

'But there was no evidence,' continued Dora. 'You arrested me for no reason.'

'I know you stole that lady's handbag,' said the constable. 'People saw you do it. But you'd thrown it away before I got hold of you.'

'Thrown it away? Where?'

'You tell me.'

Dora sighed. On that occasion, Constable Farris had been mistaken. But she had to steal, it was the only way to feed her baby son, Jonathan.

'We think the lady who was murdered on Tower Bridge could have been the victim of a robbery,' said Detective Inspector Petty.

'I thought it was her man who did it.'

'It remains a theory. But we also think she could have been robbed and then killed by one of the many thieves who live in this area.'

'A thief wouldn't do that. I know the people round here and they wouldn't do a murder. Why would they? It's a death sentence if you get caught doing something like that.'

'I agree it would be unusual,' he said. 'But perhaps something happened? Perhaps the victim put up a fight?'

'If she'd put up a fight, then the thief would've just run off. It's more trouble than it's worth. I feel sorry for the woman what died, I truly do. And I hope you catch the person what done it. But I'm telling you now, it's not the sort of thing anyone round here would do. I'm not pretending we're all saints because we're not. But no one I know would have done that murder.'

Detective Inspector Petty's moustache bristled, as if he was giving this some thought. She hoped there wasn't a lot more he could say and that the two men would leave her in peace.

'Very well, Miss Jones,' he said. 'Thank you for your help. If you think of anything else which can help us, please call in at the station on Bermondsey Street. We'll no doubt be speaking to you and your elusive friends again soon.'

'I'm already looking forward to it, sir.'

The baby stirred shortly after the police had left and Dora unbuttoned her blouse to feed him. She wasn't looking forward to the detective returning, and she knew her friends wouldn't be happy to speak to him. But there was one friend she suspected wouldn't be around.

Lizzie Clarke.

She had gone missing on the night of the murder and Dora had no idea where she was.

Chapter 8

THE CLOUDY SKY was darkening as Augusta stepped out of Mark Lane station. She walked through Trinity Square Gardens and crossed the road to where the Tower of London nestled within its thick stone walls. The ancient fortress was surrounded by a deep, wide ditch which had once served as a moat. The building fascinated her. It had stood here for more than a thousand years while London had grown and sprawled around it.

She followed the perimeter of the moat until the two towers of Tower Bridge loomed into view. Although the bridge was only thirty years old, its turrets, crenelations and mullioned windows reminded Augusta of a medieval castle. The stone and brickwork were just cladding around a structure of steel girders, but this didn't ruin her fondness for the bridge. For her, its ornate stonework evoked another era, a fairy tale even. The little windows in the arches and towers made her long to be on the other side of them, looking out.

The breeze was stronger on the bridge and it brought sleet with it. Augusta held onto her hat as she began to walk across. The north tower of the bridge loomed over her, and traffic passed beneath its wide arch. She paused and looked west to London Bridge. Beyond the thick, dark clouds, the sun had already set. She could see the cranes in the wharves on the southern bank and there were boats by the wharves of the northern bank, outside Billingsgate Market and Custom House. Looking east, she could see the warehouses of London's vast docklands which stretched out to Wapping, Shadwell, Rotherhithe, Poplar, Millwall and beyond.

Once she was past the tower, Augusta walked along the section of the bridge which lifted to make way for tall ships. Above her, two narrow walkways linked the towers and provided access between them when the road section was raised.

Augusta wondered where Celia Hawkins had been attacked. She thought of the dark and the driving rain that night. There couldn't have been many people here at the time. She stopped again and rested her hand on the wall which separated her from the river below. It was waist height. Whoever had pushed Celia Hawkins from here had mustered up some strength to achieve it.

Peering over the edge, she watched the deep river flowing swiftly beneath her. It was heading eastwards which suggested the tide was going out.

Who had the assailant been? The newspapers had reported that Celia had been robbed on the bridge a few months previously. Could the thief have been the same person who murdered her? It seemed strange that Celia had been attacked on the bridge twice.

Augusta wondered where Celia had been going on the night of her murder. She had lived and worked in Battersea, some distance from here. So where had she been travelling from and where had she been going?

Her questions were hard to answer and suddenly it seemed foolish to be standing on the bridge trying to establish what had happened. Augusta hadn't known Celia Hawkins, so there seemed little need for her to give the murder much thought. But the incident reminded her of the murders in Bloomsbury and how she had helped Philip find the culprit. She had grown so accustomed to hearing from him when events like this happened that it was unusual to hear nothing from him at all.

Was there anything she could do? Without Philip, she suspected not. If he were here now, then he would have told her more about Celia Hawkins. In cases like this, it was important to learn as much about the victim as possible. It was usually the case that the clue to their murder lay in the details of their life. Without learning anything new, Augusta was stuck.

She continued to walk the full length of the bridge. It was almost dark now and the sleet was being blown horizontally at her. She could feel the damp soaking through her coat. There were few people about and Augusta felt a prickle on the back of her neck as she thought of someone creeping up on her. What if Celia Hawkins's killer patrolled this bridge looking for new victims? She knew the thought was silly, but it wasn't completely irrational.

She turned now, keen to get back across the bridge and to the light and warmth of the tube station. Sleet found its way into her eyes and the cold stung her face. She walked briskly, heading for the lights at the far end of the bridge. But just as she reached the south tower, a bell sounded, and a uniformed man pulled a gate across the road. The bridge was closing so a ship could pass through. There was nothing Augusta could do but wait.

Now she was going to get colder and wetter. How long

was this likely to take? The traffic was stopped next to her but there were no other pedestrians around.

A movement at the base of the tower made her startle. A thief hiding in the shadows?

She didn't wait around to find out. Augusta turned and ran in the direction of Bermondsey. To her relief, she saw a bus waiting in the stopped traffic. She dashed towards it and hopped onto the little platform at the back.

Chapter 9

TOMMY PUSHED OPEN the door of the Falcon Tavern and breathed in the comforting smell of beer and tobacco. He strolled through the bar and climbed a narrow wooden staircase to a corridor with creaky floorboards. He pushed open the second door on the right and found everyone in there, sitting around a table in a cloud of cigarette smoke. The tall, grimy window overlooked Battersea's St John's Hill.

He had heard noisy chatter before entering the room, but now it was quiet. Everyone watched as he took his seat, and he felt his stomach tense. The welcome was usually much cheerier than this, but Celia's death had changed everything.

'Evening,' he said as chirpily as possible. Everyone muttered their reply. 'Is everyone here?' More muttering suggested they were. 'Good, I'll begin. Now, as you know, next Thursday is the day. George knows his drill, so we're all ready to go. We're heading for a little yard called Robin Hood Yard, which is between Hatton Garden and Leather

Lane. We've got to be there for ten o'clock. That's the time a door will accidentally be left unlocked. George will be in Ye Olde Mitre pub for fifteen minutes. When he returns, he'll realise he's accidentally left a door unlocked and will lock it again. It's likely the management will discover some jewellery has gone missing the following day, but by then we'll be in Kent. Now, let me go over again what everyone's doing. We haven't got long on the evening, only fifteen minutes. And there will be a few people about, even at ten o'clock at night, so we've got to have our wits about us.'

'I have a question.' A wide-shouldered, thick-lipped man with a scar on one cheek raised his hand.

Tommy scowled at him, he didn't like interruptions. 'What is it, Jim?'

'Do you think next Thursday is a good idea?'

'Yeah. We've had this planned for months.'

'I don't mean we shouldn't do it, but maybe we should… delay it.'

'Why?'

'Well, because of what's happened.'

It was clear that Jim was referring to Celia's murder. Tommy felt his fists clench. 'What's happened has nothing to do with the job next Thursday.'

Jim didn't reply, but a sharp-featured man with a scrappy moustache spoke up. 'Jim's got a point,' he said. 'You've got the coppers looking at you, Tommy. We should wait until everything's calmed down. And Billy will be out soon so maybe—'

'They may be looking at me, Frank, but I've not done nothing wrong. We all know that, don't we? They've got nothing on me. Of course, they're going to hassle me about it, but that's all done with, anyway. I've told them what I know. And I know nothing about it.'

'But they might be watching you,' said Jim. 'And if they're watching you, they might find out about the job.'

Tommy gritted his teeth. He had been working on this for months and it was his chance to prove he could run a job of this scale. With Billy in prison, everyone now looked to Tommy instead. He and Billy had known each other since their school days. Not that either of them had attended school too often, they had been out and about trying to find money for their families instead. Tommy's father had been in prison and a man who worked on the railways had moved into the family home in his place. He'd taken his temper out on Tommy and his younger brothers. When he turned thirteen, Tommy had fought back and broken the man's nose.

Billy had never known his father, and his mother had been a drinker. For as long as Tommy could remember, the pair of them had roamed the streets of south London, stealing from shops and picking pockets.

Tommy hadn't been conscripted during the war because he had a hernia. Billy had avoided conscription too because he had a weak chest. The pair had worked in a munitions factory filling bullets and shells with yellow TNT powder. They got covered in so much of the stuff that their faces went yellow and they were nicknamed canaries. They had shared a lot. They were as close as brothers.

Billy had been in charge because everyone feared him. He had arranged a job in Bond Street the previous year and Tommy had helped him, acting as his second in command. Billy had told him he had done well and clearly told the boss this. The boss was happy for him to run the Hatton Garden job while Billy was in prison. As the organiser, Tommy had been promised the biggest share. After the boss, of course.

But today there was dissent, and Tommy had to

somehow assert his authority. Having stepped into Billy's shoes, he felt out of his depth. He was a good fighter and could take down any of them with no problem at all. But when he was up against eight people, that was a different story.

He had to insist on the job taking place. To back down or change his mind looked like weakness. He was the one in charge, and he had to remind them of that.

'If we don't do next Thursday, we can't do it at all,' he snapped.

'Why not?' said Frank.

'Because I can't tell you how much work it took to get George to go along with this. He was nervous about getting involved. If we change it now, he'll get cold feet. We'll lose him and we'll have to start all over again. I don't think any of you here realise how much I've put into this.'

'We realise it,' said Frank. 'We know you work hard, Tommy. Harder than anyone else I know. But I'm with Jim, if you've caught the eye of the coppers for something else—'

'Which I didn't do.'

'And I believe you, Tommy, you didn't do it. But the coppers are asking you questions all the same because you and Celia was together. So you're in their minds now, wrongly, I know. But that's what the situation is. And I think we're all worried that if the job goes ahead next Thursday, the police might find out. They could have someone watching you and following you about.'

'I've not seen no one following me about.'

'What if they're good at it?'

Tommy gave a snort. 'The coppers are good at nothing. That's why they've been asking me questions! They've not got the first idea who did that to Celia.'

It was the first time he had said her name in front of

them, and it seemed strange. It seemed too personal. He lit a cigarette and addressed Frank. 'What did you mean when you said that you're *all* worried about the job going ahead next Thursday. Is that what everyone in here thinks?'

No one spoke, but heads nodded subtly.

'So you do all think that? No one's brave enough to admit it, other than Jim and Frank?'

He felt a bitter taste in his mouth, they weren't scared enough of him. Was he losing their support? This wasn't a good sign. But it meant, more than ever, that next week's job had to go ahead. He had to do it while they were still behind him. In another few weeks, who knew where he would be?

'I've listened to you,' he said. 'But I know we can pull it off. Between us, we've got a lot of experience. I can't waste all the preparation we've done for this. The plans are finalised and George is all set to go. I think you lot are getting too nervy.'

'We're trying to be sensible about it,' said Frank.

'Sensible? Since when was any of us sensible? The job's going ahead next Thursday, like we planned. Now I don't want no more complaining about it.'

He had said it and they had to listen to him. He needed this job more than he had ever needed anything. He needed the money, and he needed the distraction.

Anything to help him stop thinking about Celia.

Chapter 10

'THERE IS no answer on that telephone at the moment,' said the switchboard operator.

'Alright then, thank you.' Augusta replaced her telephone receiver. This was the third time she had telephoned Philip and the third time there had been no answer. She sighed and returned to her workshop where a copy of George Eliot's *Middlemarch* lay on the worktable.

She picked up the book and smiled as she read the inscription on the front flyleaf.

To a dear friend, on the occasion of his birthday. May this book bring you much joy.

The author of the message had signed off as Timothy and the date was June 1899. Augusta wondered where Timothy was now. And who had been the friend he had given the book to?

Whoever he was, he had looked after the book well. The cover needed only minor repairs, and none of the page corners had been turned down. Had the friend even read it?

A knock sounded at the door and Fred peered in. 'Mrs Peel, there's someone here to see you.' He pulled a grimace.

'Not Mr Fairburn again?'

'No, someone else.'

'Thank you, Fred.' She put the book down and followed him into the shop.

A young man in a tweed suit stood by the counter. Augusta recognised him as the agent who had shown her around the shop before she took on the tenancy. He held a clipboard and gave her a weak smile.

'Good morning, Mrs Peel. I'm Bertie Elman. We've met before.'

'We have. How can I help?'

'We've had a report which I'm obliged to follow up on, I'm afraid.'

'What sort of report?'

'There's been a suggestion of unscrupulous business practices.'

Augusta gave a groan. 'Did the suggestion come from Mr Fairburn of Webster's bookshop, by any chance?'

'I'm not permitted to say where the complaint has come from.'

'So it's a complaint rather than a suggestion?'

'Yes, it is a complaint, Mrs Peel.'

'And what have we supposedly done wrong?' asked Fred, his hands on his hips.

'A few things.' He consulted some papers on his clip-board. 'Firstly, there is a question over whether approval was granted for a bookshop to be opened on these premises.'

'Did I not mention to you my plans for a bookshop when you showed me around this place?'

'I can't remember.'

'Neither can I. So is approval required?'

'I don't know.'

'Well, as neither of us can remember if approval was given, let's just say it was. That would be easier, wouldn't it?'

He tapped his pen on his chin as he thought about this. 'Alright then. We'll say approval was granted.' He made some notes.

'Thank you. What else?'

'Secondly, a complaint about garish signage which isn't in keeping with the tone of the other shops in this area.'

'Did you see any garish signage on the front of my shop when you arrived just now, Mr Elman?'

'No, I must admit I didn't. Perhaps the complainant is referring to temporary signage, which can sometimes be garish in nature.'

'Can it?'

'Temporary signage is often used when there is a discount of some sort in the shop. Have you held any discounting sales recently?'

'No. My books are already a good price because they're second-hand. I think that's what Mr Fairburn takes issue with.'

'I see. Thirdly, apparently there are animals on the premises.' He pointed at the birdcage. 'I'm assuming he means the budgerigar.'

'Canary,' corrected Augusta.

'Any other animals?' asked the agent.

'No,' replied Fred. 'Unless you count the giraffe we keep in the workshop at the back.'

'Giraffe?'

'Mr Plummer was joking,' said Augusta, amused by the agent's baffled expression. 'There are no animals here

43

other than a canary. He's here during the day and then I take him home with me in the evening.'

'I see.'

'I take it that a canary in a cage is permitted?'

'Yes. When I first read the complaint, I assumed there were several animals here.'

'I suspect that was Mr Fairburn's intention.'

'And finally, there is a report of malicious business practices.'

'Which could cover a wide variety of things. Have you got any more detail?'

'It says here there is a deliberate undercutting of prices in a manner which has a detrimental effect on the business of other bookstores in the immediate proximity.'

'Mr Fairburn is doing his best to sound as officious as possible,' said Augusta. 'What he's referring to is the fact my books are cheaper than his. And the reason for that is the fact my books are second-hand. I collect old books, then I repair them and sell them. Mr Fairburn is supplied directly by the publishing companies, so he stocks new books which are more expensive. I've already explained to him that our bookshops attract different types of customers. Those who want a new book which has recently been published can shop at his store. Those who like to read older editions, some of which have arguably more character than new books, come to my shop.'

'I see.'

'Mr Fairburn has already visited me and complained about this shop and I've done my best to explain all this to him. But he still resents my presence here and so he's contacted your agency with some complaints which, quite frankly, are a waste of your time.'

'I didn't realise Mr Fairburn has already spoken directly to you about these matters.'

'Yes, he has. And he's probably disappointed that his visit had no effect. That's why he contacted you. He clearly has no respect for your time, Mr Elman. He's merely involved you as part of his plan to have me evicted from my shop. Is the landlord, Sir Pritchard, aware you're here today?'

'Not yet. Although I shall report my findings to him.'

'He and I share a mutual friend, Lady Hereford.'

The agent lowered his clipboard. 'Is that so? I think I remember that now.'

'She's a very good friend of mine. In fact, Sparky the canary belongs to her. I've been looking after Sparky while she's endured a period of ill health.'

'She's been unwell? I'm sorry to hear it.'

'I'm sure both she and Sir Pritchard would be disappointed to hear about your visit today.'

'Possibly.'

'They might wonder if Mr Fairburn's concerns could have been dealt with in a manner which didn't require you to visit us with your clipboard.'

'They might.'

Augusta hoped he was now regretting his visit. 'Is there anything else on your list that you'd like to discuss with us, Mr Elman?'

'No, I think that's all.'

'So your report to the landlord will be favourable?'

'There's probably no need for me to make any report at all. Everything here appears to be in order.'

'Thank you, Mr Elman.'

'No, thank you for your time, Mrs Peel. And Mr Plummer.'

'Perhaps reply to Mr Fairburn that each of his claims is entirely unfounded and you suspect they've been made out of malice rather than being based on any fact?'

'I think that suggestion could be made to him, yes.'

'Thank you. And if he makes another complaint, then perhaps you could reply to that effect rather than bothering us?'

'I think that's entirely possible, Mrs Peel.'

Chapter 11

THREE OTHER GUESTS were staying at the lodging house on Southampton Row, and they were all men. There was an older gentleman who wore the same grey cardigan every day and spent his time reading *The Sporting Times*. He liked to discuss horse racing with another lodger, who was an insurance salesman with oily hair. The third gentleman was Mrs Flynn's favourite, a foppish fair-haired man called Rupert, who was trying to find work as an actor. It was a habit of the landlady to sit at his breakfast table every morning and read the newspaper to him. Mary kept to herself and felt pleased the other four didn't bother her too much.

In the shop, she spent the first few days organising the stock in the storeroom. Mrs Saunders told her it was the best way to learn about everything they sold. Mary was given a logbook in which she could note all the sacks and boxes they had of each product. Mrs Saunders had told her it would take two days, but Mary had finished it by lunchtime on the second day.

'Are you sure you've made a note of everything?' said Mrs Saunders.

'Yes.'

The manager took the logbook into the storeroom and carried out a few checks. Five minutes later, she seemed happy. 'You've done a very good job, Mary, well done. And it looks tidier in there too. Did you sweep the floor?'

'Yes.'

'Well done. You're ready to work with Lucy behind the counter now.'

Mary enjoyed her work, it distracted her from the past. But she felt uncomfortable when Lucy asked her questions. 'Why did you leave Bournemouth?' she asked.

'I wanted to see London.'

'Why?'

'There's more going on here.'

'Like what?'

'There are all the famous sights which I want to see.'

'They're easy to see in a few day trips. I don't see why you'd move here to see them. Bournemouth is by the sea, isn't it?'

'Yes, it is.'

'You've got healthy, clean air down there. Didn't you know how dirty the air is in London? Sometimes the fog is so thick and filthy you can hardly see your hand in front of your face.'

'I didn't realise it got that bad.'

'I'd happily leave London, given half the chance,' said Lucy.

'Why don't you?'

'I've got all my family here. I don't want to be on my own somewhere. I don't know anyone who lives in the country or by the sea. Are your family in Bournemouth?'

'Yes.'

'And you had a job there?'

'Yes. I worked in a cafe.'

'I don't know why you left. You might realise before long that it would've been a better idea to stay there.'

'Perhaps I will.'

'What did your family say when you told them you were coming to London?'

'They thought it was a good idea.'

'Really? My ma wouldn't let me move too far away. And I have to give her some of my wages. Do you send anything back to your family?'

'A little.'

'There's no more money to be made in London than there is anywhere else, not unless you become a dancing girl in one of the nightclubs. You can earn good money in the West End doing that sort of thing. I've got some friends who do it.'

'I've got no interest in doing that.'

'You're going to be a shopgirl until you find a husband?'

'I think so.'

'Have you got brothers? Sisters?'

'A sister.'

'Just one?'

'Yes.'

'Is she older or younger?'

'Younger.' Mary didn't like talking about herself. 'Where do your family live?' she asked, keen to change the conversation.

Thankfully, Lucy seemed happy to talk. 'My family lives in Hammersmith and that's where I was born,' she said. 'I've got two older sisters and a younger brother. One sister's married and lives with her husband and two children in the same house as my parents. Her family live downstairs and Ma and Pa and my brother live upstairs. My other sister lives in a house with a friend in Chiswick. They both work in Fuller's brewery. My brother works in the soap factory. I've got lodgings in Holborn because I didn't want to stay in Hammersmith. My parents didn't even want me moving this far away from them! It's only six miles, and they weren't happy about it. I wanted to move away and be independent, but it's not as far as you've come.'

An elderly man strolled into the shop with a spaniel on a lead.

'Half a pound of Spratt's dog biscuits, please.'

'Of course,' said Lucy. She glanced at the sacks of dog biscuits. 'Oh that one's empty. We don't have any left. The delivery's been delayed.'

'None left? What's my dog going to eat?'

'Some other biscuits?'

'But he only likes Spratt's.'

'We can't help. Sorry.'

'Well, that's a shame indeed, you've always been so good in this store. I've never known you to run out of something before.'

Mary felt sure she had seen a bag of Spratt's dog biscuits in the storeroom. As the man turned to leave, she couldn't resist speaking out.

'I'll check out the back,' she said. 'I think I saw a bag in there.'

Lucy gave her an icy stare. But the man was grateful. 'Oh, would you? Thank you, young lady.'

She found the bag in the storeroom, picked it up and carried it into the shop. Lucy didn't help at all as Mary weighed out the biscuits, tipped them into a paper bag, twisted over the top and placed it on the counter.

'Thank you so much for your help,' said the man, handing over threepence.

An uncomfortable silence remained between Mary and Lucy after he left the shop.

Chapter 12

'I THOUGHT you dealt with that agent very well earlier, Mrs Peel,' said Fred.

Augusta picked up the bag of bird food and fed a few seeds to Sparky. 'Thank you. It took some effort to remain calm. I can't believe he didn't challenge Mr Fairburn about his claims before turning up here.'

'I think he will do next time.'

'I hope so. Although there shouldn't be a next time.'

A shiny black car pulled up outside the shop.

'Look at that!' said Fred. 'A Daimler!'

'How can you tell?'

'I just know.'

The pair of them watched as the chauffeur got out and opened the door for a well-dressed man in a top hat.

'It looks like he's going to come in here!' said Fred. 'I'll open the door for him.'

Augusta smiled as Fred skipped to the door and opened it for the gentleman.

'Thank you, young man.' He strolled into the shop,

tapping a gold-topped cane on the floor. He wore a fur-trimmed overcoat over a smart black suit.

'Good afternoon,' he said to Augusta in a clipped voice. He looked about forty, and his dark moustache was waxed at the ends.

Augusta returned the greeting. 'Are you looking for anything in particular?' she asked.

'Some Sherlock Holmes stories. Do you have any?'

'Yes, we do. Any particular one?'

'*The Hound of the Baskervilles*, if you have it. I borrowed it from the library recently and enjoyed it so much that I was rather put out I had to return it. I'd like a copy for myself.'

'Yes, we have it.' Augusta walked over to the shelf which held all the books by Arthur Conan Doyle. The gentleman joined her.

'I see you have *A Study in Scarlet* too! Excellent, I'll take that. And what's this?' He took down a blue bound book from the shelf. '*Ghost Stories and Presentiments*,' he said. 'What a nice cover.' He stroked the gold lettering and Augusta noticed his long, elegant fingers. 'Has this book been restored?'

'Yes, it has. It was published in 1888.'

'So it's over thirty years old. Well, it's in marvellous condition. I'll take this one too.'

Augusta took the three books over to the counter.

'Now I'm not finished yet,' said the gentleman. 'Have you got anything by Thomas Hardy? A completely different sort of chap to Conan Doyle, but enjoyable all the same.'

'I've just restored a copy of *Jude the Obscure*.'

'You've restored it?'

'Yes.'

'Did you restore all these books?'

'Yes.'

A smile spread across his face. 'Well, that's impressive indeed! Let me take a look at the Thomas Hardy shelf.'

A little while later, the gentleman left with twelve books. Fred helped him carry them out to his car.

'Let's hope Mr Fairburn didn't notice him,' said Fred when the car had driven away. 'He'll be angry he called in here instead of Webster's.'

'Good. And for that reason, I hope he did notice him!' They laughed. 'Now because he spent a good amount of money, I think we can afford to close early, Fred.'

'No. Really?'

'I need to go somewhere.'

'Where?'

'It sounds silly, but I want to carry on searching for Detective Inspector Fisher. I still don't understand why there's been no word from him and I'd like to call at his home.'

'That's a good idea. You go and do that, Mrs Peel, and I'll mind the shop.'

'We can close early, then you can go home.'

'Never close early. You never know who might be planning to visit today.'

'I see. Well, thank you Fred. I'm impressed by your attitude to work.'

'I hope you find the detective inspector, Mrs Peel.'

'So do I.'

An hour later, it was dusk as Augusta walked along a street of terraced houses in Willesden. It was a respectable street just a short walk from the railway station. Each house had a neat little front garden bordered by railings. Augusta stopped at number twenty-four. It had a red door and a tiled path led up to the doorstep. The curtains in the bay window were drawn, as were the curtains in the two upper floor windows. Had there been a bereavement?

If so, then coming here was probably a mistake. But it seemed wrong to walk away again without trying the doorbell.

Augusta took in a breath and walked up to the door and pressed the bell. She heard it echo within the house, but there was no further sound. The door had a little semi-circular window at the top, which she had no hope of being tall enough to peer into.

A motor car drove past, but everything else seemed quiet. She felt sure the house was empty. There was no one at home. What had happened to Philip and his family? It was time to call on a neighbour.

Augusta knocked on the door of number twenty-two. A young woman holding a child answered. She wore an apron and had flour on her face. 'Can I help?'

'I hope so. I'm a friend of your neighbour, Philip Fisher. But I haven't heard from him in a while, so I thought I'd call on him. There doesn't appear to be anyone at home. Have you seen him recently?'

'Not since before Christmas.'

'Really?'

'I think they've gone to stay with Audrey's mother.'

'Oh.'

'I know he works as a policeman, so I'm surprised he's gone too, because you'd think he'd be needed at Scotland Yard. But perhaps he's unwell and they've gone for a change of air?'

'Perhaps. Did they tell you a reason?'

'No, they seemed to leave in a hurry. I saw Audrey and Michael getting into a car and they had some suitcases with them. I didn't see Philip. I asked her if she was going anywhere nice and she said she was going to her mother's. She wasn't very talkative, which is unlike her. We've always got on well. And that was several weeks ago. I can only guess they'll be back soon. I know I wouldn't want to stay with my mother for that long!' She laughed.

Augusta smiled. 'Do you know where Audrey's mother lives?'

'Somewhere on the south coast. I think it could be Worthing or Littlehampton.'

'I see.' It was frustrating that the neighbour was unable to narrow it down any further. She thanked the neighbour and turned to leave.

'Would you like me to pass on a message when they return?' the neighbour called out.

'Thank you. I don't know Audrey, I've not met her. But I've worked with Philip in the past. If you see him, can you let him know that Augusta Peel called on him?'

'Of course.'

Augusta walked back to the railway station, wondering why Philip and his family had gone to the south coast. Although she felt disappointed he hadn't told her he was going away, she knew it was foolish to fret about it. Clearly, he didn't consider them to be close enough friends to mention it, and that seemed sensible.

She took in a breath and told herself to forget about him for now. He was with his family, and there was no need for her to worry about him.

And there was certainly no need for her to miss him as much as she did.

Chapter 13

Tommy Barnes walked along Fleet Street, dodging the people hurrying to work.

Tommy was in less of a hurry. He'd been summoned to see the boss, and he was nervous. An early morning murky fog hung low over the rooftops and Tommy shoved his chilly hands into the pockets of his smart trousers. He was wearing his Sunday best, even though it was Tuesday.

He reached the newspaper offices sooner than he would have liked. Signs on the front of the building advertised the *Morning Express* and *Evening Gazette*.

Tommy stopped at the shiny door. Before he rang the bell, he rubbed the toe of each shoe on the back of his trouser legs. Then he took off his cap and smoothed his hair.

A young man in a smart suit answered the door.

'The name's Barnes,' said Tommy.

'He's expecting you.' The young man was a similar age to Tommy but spoke with an accent as sharp as cut glass. Tommy guessed he had probably attended a posh school.

The young man stepped to one side to allow him in. 'Do you know where his office is?'

'Yes thank you, I've visited him here before.'

He could hear the rumble of printing presses from somewhere in the building. A man dashed past them, a pencil behind his ear. He muttered a greeting to the smart young man and rushed upstairs.

Tommy climbed the staircase, his heart thudding as he did so. The boss met with the gang members only when it was necessary. He kept them at arm's length for most of the time and sent messages via messenger boys. Tommy felt worried but knew he had to do all he could to show he was confident. If he had confidence in himself, then the boss would have confidence in him too.

He found the door and gave it an assertive knock.

'Come in.'

Tommy turned the handle and stepped into the room. The large windows overlooked Fleet Street and were framed by royal blue velvet curtains. An oriental rug covered the floor and a large desk was positioned at one end of the room. An ornate fireplace with a lively fire in the grate was at the other end of the room and the boss sat in an easy chair there.

'Tommy.' He gave a smile. 'Come and join me by the fire.' He had been reading a book, which he now rested on a side table. As Tommy took a seat in another easy chair, he saw the book was *The Hound of the Baskervilles*. He liked the sound of the story and fancied reading it himself. He hadn't attended school very often, but he had learned to read.

'How are you Tommy?'

'I'm well, thank you, sir.' As much as he tried to feel confident, he couldn't help but feel cowed in the man's presence. His mouth and throat felt dry.

'I'm sorry to hear about your wife.'

'We weren't married, but we lived as man and wife. Thank you.'

'It must have been a dreadful shock.'

'It was.'

'Have you been interviewed by the police?'

'I have.'

'How many times?'

'Just once.'

'And what did you tell them?'

'The truth.'

'I see. Are you in the habit of telling the police the truth?'

'Not at all.'

'They've interviewed you in the past regarding other incidents, haven't they?'

'They have, sir. I know how to handle myself with the police.'

'I suppose when they interviewed you about Celia, they were aware of the other occasions you've crossed their path?'

'They were.'

'Did they mention those other occasions?'

'No, not really.'

'Not really?'

'Just in passing. They want to catch Celia's killer and I hope they do.'

'So do I.'

He lit a cigar and puffed out a plume of smoke. 'Do you know why I've invited you here today, Tommy?'

'No.'

'Would you like to guess?'

'I wouldn't like to guess, sir.' He didn't want to risk saying anything which could antagonise the gentleman.

'Very well. I shall just come out with it then. There are some reservations about the job on Thursday.'

Tommy clenched his teeth. Someone had spoken to Sir Charles. But who? Perhaps it had been Frank. Or maybe Jim.

'I also understand those reservations were expressed to you. Am I right?'

'Yes, you're right.'

'There is some concern that the recent events regarding your poor wife, Celia, create an element of risk. The police could be watching you.'

'I feel sure the police aren't watching me.'

'You may well feel sure, Tommy, but we have to be extremely careful. The tragic incident has put a spotlight on you somewhat. And although I'm sure you're entirely innocent of any wrongdoing, the recent attention from the police puts the attention on you, so to speak. You're no doubt fairly prominent in their minds. And that's a risk I'd rather not take.'

Disappointment niggled at him. 'With all due respect, sir, I feel strongly that the job must go ahead. It took a lot of work to persuade the man on the inside to do it.'

'I'm sure it did.'

'And I'm worried that if there's any delay to the job, he'll use it as an excuse to back out. He's already nervous about it as it is.'

'Yes, I'm sure he is. It's often the way. And I appreciate the amount of work you've put into this.'

'I believe it's what I'm good at, sir.'

'And I believe that, too. Billy has always spoken highly of you. However, I think the concerns about the job are not without foundation.'

'But sir, if we don't do the job on Thursday, then it

might not happen at all. We're set to make a lot of money from it.'

'I couldn't agree more. And I'm not suggesting the job shouldn't go ahead. Instead, Tommy, I'm asking you to step aside and allow the rest of the men to do it.'

His heart sank.

'Without me? How? I've organised it all!'

'You have indeed. And that's why I feel it would be quite easy for Frank to take over.'

Frank! He was the snake in the grass.

'But the inside man has been dealing with me, sir. I don't think he'll trust Frank.'

'He will if you make the proper introductions.'

'I think he'll get suspicious. He'll wonder why I'm leaving the job.'

'Then you'll have to do your best to persuade him that all is well, Tommy. It sounds like you've done a good job with him so far.'

Despair consumed him, and he tried desperately to keep calm. He wanted to march over to Sir Charles and shake him by the collar until he could make him see sense. But that was no good, he had to remain polite and deferential. He would ruin everything for himself if he lost control.

But he was being pushed out, and it wasn't right.

'I realise you're disappointed to hear this, Tommy,' said Sir Charles. 'But I have to consider everyone else and the job itself. This business with your wife has made you a liability, I'm afraid. You know what they say about mud sticking.'

Why did Sir Charles keep calling her his wife? He wondered now if Sir Charles thought he had harmed Celia. Is that why he wanted to distance himself from him?

And who was Sir Charles, anyway? Just a rich man

who had lots of people doing his dirty work for him. The man was set to make even more money off the back of Tommy's hard work. It wasn't fair.

But Tommy had to accept it, even if every bone in his body told him not to. 'Alright,' he said. 'I'm still part of it though, aren't I?'

'Part of it?'

'Part of the gang. It's like family to me. It's all I've ever known.' His voice cracked as he said these last words and he felt immediate shame. It was weak, and Sir Charles could tell it was weak. He felt sure the man was regarding him with contempt now.

Sir Charles inhaled on his cigar and blew out a cloud of smoke. 'I know where to find you, Tommy. I'll be in touch again when the time is right.'

Minutes later, Tommy stormed along Fleet Street, unaware of where he was going. He walked fast. His arms swinging, his fists clenched.

He felt rage. Pure rage. He needed to punch something. He *had* to punch something. A sign stood outside a shop. He pulled his arm back and drove his fist into the centre of it. The force sent it clattering several yards down the street. People stared. A man opened his mouth to remonstrate, but the expression on Tommy's face clearly made him think better of it.

He strode on and reached a greengrocer's shop. With a shout, he swung his foot at the legs of a vegetable display. Crates of potatoes tumbled to the ground, and he felt a release of tension. This was good. It was even funny. It was making him feel better.

A delivery bicycle leant against a wall. He grabbed it and swung it around, hurling it into the road with a clatter.

A bus beeped its horn, and he heard shouts. He marched on. If anyone dared confront him, they would regret it.

And someone did. A man blocked his way. A big mistake. He stood taller than Tommy, but that didn't worry him. He pulled his arm back and drove forward with his fist.

Chapter 14

DORA JONES DECIDED she had to find Lizzie. She had been missing for a week now. She wrapped her baby son in blankets, placed him in the old perambulator she had found abandoned near Guy's Hospital and made the journey over Tower Bridge to the north side of the Thames. Once over the bridge, she continued up to Mansell Street on the edge of the City of London, passed beneath the railway bridges, then turned right into Great Prescot Street before turning left again into a grid of narrow streets, clustered with little townhouses.

She had visited Lizzie's family with her a few times and couldn't remember the exact house they lived in. Neither could she read the street signs or the numbers on the doors. So she called at the nearest house and, fortunately, the lady who answered knew Lizzie's family.

'You want number fifteen.' She pointed to a house which looked familiar now that it had been pointed out to her. Dora thanked the lady for her help and went off to call at it.

Mrs Clarke, Lizzie's mother, answered. Her hair was

grey, her face was gaunt and her speech a little slurred. She didn't appear to recognise Dora from her previous visits. She looked at the baby in the perambulator. 'I've not got no money if that's what you're after.'

'No, I'm not after that at all. I've come to see Lizzie.'

'Lizzie?' The woman squinted a little, then widened her eyes as if suddenly remembering who her daughter was. 'Oh, Lizzie. I've not seen her.'

'Has she not been here recently?'

'Recently?' Mrs Clarke laughed. 'I've not seen her in years!'

This wasn't true because Dora recalled visiting Mrs Clarke with Lizzie about a year previously.

'I've not seen Lizzie for a week,' said Dora. 'And I'm worried about her.'

'I wouldn't worry. She'll be back when she needs money.'

'I live in the same flat as her and it's unusual for her to go missing.'

'I wouldn't say it was. But having said that, I'm the last person on earth she'd visit!' She cackled.

'Don't you remember me visiting you with Lizzie about a year ago?'

'You visited me, did you? Don't remember. You must be mistaken.'

'We definitely did.'

'Well, I'm sorry I've forgotten you. My mind's not what it was. Won't be long before I forget all my children!' She laughed again and Dora doubted she would get much sense from her.

'Who are you talking to, Ma?' came a young woman's voice from the dingy hallway.

'A friend of Lizzie's.'

A girl of about fourteen pushed past her mother and

surveyed Dora. Her face was thin and her front two teeth protruded.

'I'm Dora.'

'I'm Hetty, I remember you.' She looked down into the perambulator. 'You've got a baby!' A smile spread across her face. 'Boy or a girl?'

'A boy. Jonathan.'

Mrs Clarke appeared to give up on the conversation and retreated into her home.

'Aw, look at him sleeping peacefully,' said Hetty.

'He knows how to make a noise when he wants to,' said Dora with a smile. 'I'm looking for Lizzie. I live in the same flat as her and I've not seen her for a while. Have you?'

The girl shook her head. 'I think she came round about two weeks ago. Maybe three weeks. But I've not seen her since then.'

'Alright, I'll keep looking. Your mother seems to think she hasn't seen her in years.'

Hetty smiled. 'She thinks like that sometimes. She gets confused.'

'How was Lizzie when you saw her?'

'Just normal Lizzie.'

'Have you got any idea where she could've gone?'

'No.'

'Alright then, I'll keep asking around and see if I can find her.'

The girl's brow crumpled. 'Are you worried about her?'

'Worried? No, I'm not worried.' The girl was only young and Dora didn't want to concern her if Lizzie then turned out to be safe and well. 'I'll try somewhere else. Thank you for your help.'

'When you see her, can you tell her to visit us?' said Hetty. 'I'm worried Ma is getting worse.'

'I will.' Dora attempted to give her a reassuring smile.

There was someone else Dora could speak to about Lizzie's disappearance and she wasn't keen to see him. But she felt the need to do what she could to find her.

The Three Horns was a shabby pub near St Saviour's Dock in Bermondsey. Dora took baby Jonathan from his perambulator and held him close as she pushed open the door. Noisy laughter and cigarette smoke greeted her. It was hot and there were few women about. Dora cuddled her son to her chest as she ignored the remarks from leering men. She caught sight of Robbie Winchcombe at the back of the pub. He wasn't difficult to miss with his broad shoulders, thick jaw and broken nose. He stood with a group of men and their lively chatter stopped as they noticed her approach.

'Well, if it isn't Dora,' he said. His fat lips pushed into a smile.

'I'm looking for Lizzie,' she said. 'Have you seen her?'

'Probably at her ma's,' he replied. 'Too frightened to show me her face for a few days!' He snickered, and his cronies joined in. Dora shuddered, not wishing to think too much about the meaning behind his words. She had done her best to persuade Lizzie to stay away from Robbie, but she seemed unable to.

'She's not at her ma's,' she shouted over the laughter.

'I don't know where she is. She'll show her face soon enough. Stay for a drink, Dora, you look like you need cheering up.'

'I'm worried about Lizzie.'

'That's what she wants you to do. She wants everyone worrying about her. She loves the attention. That's why I ignore her half the time!' Dora sneered at him and turned to leave. He grabbed her arm and pushed his face close to hers. He was sweaty and stank of beer. 'Stay for a drink, Dora.'

His grip on her arm was hard, but she gave the skin on the back of his hand a hard pinch and he released his grip.

'I can't stay,' she said. 'I need to feed my baby.'

'Give him some beer!' said one of Robbie's friends. 'Get him started young!'

They laughed as she pushed her way out of the pub as quickly as she could.

Chapter 15

'You need to come down from there, Sparky,' said Augusta. 'It's your bedtime.' The canary sat on the curtain rail and ignored her.

Lady Hereford had introduced a routine for Sparky which Augusta attempted to impose with various degrees of success. Between the hours of nine in the evening and seven in the morning, he was supposed to roost in his large cage with a silk shawl draped over it. Lady Hereford believed a routine was essential for a contented canary, and it seemed to work. Unless Sparky refused to go to bed.

A knock sounded at the door and Augusta caught her breath. Could it be Philip? She dashed over to the door and peered through the little peephole. A man in a bowler hat with spectacles and grey whiskers stood there.

She opened the door cautiously. 'Hello?'

'Mrs Peel.' He removed his hat. 'I'm Detective Inspector Morris of Scotland Yard. I hope you don't mind me calling on you like this.'

'Not at all. Has something happened?'

'Nothing to worry about,' he said, clearly sensing her anxiety. 'May I have a quick word?'

'Of course, come in.'

He stepped into her apartment. 'I understand you've been making enquiries about Detective Inspector Fisher.'

'Yes. Do you know where he is?'

'No.'

'Oh.'

'But I can tell you what I do know and I must add that, as a friend of Philip's, I'm concerned about him.'

'Oh no, why?'

'I last saw him five or six weeks ago.'

'That long ago?'

'I'm afraid so. He seemed rather tired and distracted. In fact, he didn't seem his usual self at all.'

'Oh no, this is worrying!'

'Yes, it is. And then, one weekend, he sent me a telegram apologising for the fact he wouldn't be coming to work on Monday. He told me he had some things to sort out and he would be back as soon as possible. But obviously, time has ticked on and there's been no word from him.'

'I called at his house yesterday,' said Augusta. 'And I spoke to his neighbour. She thinks the family is at his mother-in-law's home in Worthing or Littlehampton.'

'Bognor Regis.'

'I'm sorry?'

'That's where his mother-in-law and her husband live. His wife and son are currently staying with them, but Philip isn't.'

'So where is he?'

'I don't know.'

'But how do you know he's not in Bognor Regis?'

'Because I called on the family.'

'Do they know where he is?'

'I'm afraid they don't.'

'But they must be terribly worried about him!'

'I'm sure they are. I can only think the chap wants a bit of time to himself. However, some time has passed now and I would like to think we'll see him again soon. So if there's anywhere you can think of, Mrs Peel, where he might have gone, do let me know. Perhaps he's mentioned particular places to you in the past? There may be something which comes up when you think about it. And if it does, don't hesitate to telephone me.' He reached into his pocket and pulled out a card, which he handed to Augusta.

As she took it, she noticed her hand trembling. The fact that a colleague of Philip's was also worried about him made the matter seem more serious now.

'I hope he's alright,' she said.

'So do I. I'm sure he is. I think he just needed a break from things for some reason. But he could do with getting in touch with someone just so we know he's well.'

'I really appreciate you coming to see me, Detective Inspector Morris. If I think of somewhere he can be, then I'll let you know. And if you receive any news about him, you'll let me know too, won't you?'

'Of course.'

'And if Philip was working at the moment, then I imagine he would have been working on the case of Celia Hawkins.'

'Yes, I should think he would be. It's the sort of case he's good at and I think it's safe to say that we need him at the moment. It's in the hands of Detective Inspector Petty.'

'Has he made any progress with it?'

'Not a great deal, yet. We're hampered by the fact there are no witnesses.'

'Have you found out what she was doing on Tower Bridge on a night like that?'

'No. Her common-law husband, Mr Barnes, doesn't know what she was doing there, and the weather was inclement, as you suggest. She must have arranged to meet someone, but we don't know who. Between you and me, Mr Barnes has a violent temper. It may be that she didn't wish to tell him what she was doing or who she was meeting.'

'I see. I've read in the newspapers that Mr Barnes is a suspect.'

'He is. I think an alibi has been found for him for that night, but not all alibis turn out to be reliable. All we can do is continue with our work and see where it gets us.'

'You may know that I have helped Philip with a few cases in the past. Do let Detective Inspector Petty know that I'm happy to help if he needs it.'

'I will do, Mrs Peel.' He placed his hat on his head and readied himself to leave. 'And fingers crossed Philip turns up soon.'

Chapter 16

'WHAT HAPPENED?'

Augusta arrived at the shop the following morning to find Fred out of breath and surrounded by books scattered across the floor.

'Street urchins,' he puffed. 'I tried to catch them, but they were too fast for me.'

'They did this?'

'Yes. I'd just opened up and a group of them ran in and began pulling the books off the shelves.'

'Did they say anything?'

'No, they were just laughing. I shouted at them to stop, but they ignored me.'

Augusta felt something crunch beneath her feet and looked down. 'Is that… bird seed?'

'Yes. I grabbed the nearest thing I could throw at them and it happened to be the bag of bird seed.' He pulled an apologetic face. 'Sorry about that. It worked, and they all ran out. But the bag split and…'

'I can see what's happened.' Augusta bent down and began picking up the books off the floor.

'I don't understand it,' said Fred. 'We've never had any trouble like this before, have we?'

'No. I wonder if our friend, Mr Fairburn of Webster's bookshop sent them.'

Fred's eyes widened. 'He wouldn't do a thing like that, would he?'

'I don't know. You know him better than I do.'

'Perhaps he would. But what a thing to do! Does he think that you'll feel so threatened by it you'll close the shop?'

'I think so. What a foolish man, he doesn't know me at all. Are any of the books damaged?'

'This copy of *Jane Eyre* has a ripped spine.'

Augusta stepped over and examined it. 'That should be easy enough to fix. Why don't you fetch the broom and I'll pick up the rest of the books.'

As they tidied up, Augusta told Fred about the visit from Detective Inspector Morris the previous evening. 'I don't understand why no one knows where Philip is,' she added. 'You'd have thought he would have confided in someone.'

'Perhaps he has.'

'But I can't think who. I don't remember him mentioning the names of any friends to me.'

'That doesn't mean he doesn't have friends.'

'True.'

'And Detective Inspector Morris is only a colleague of his, so he probably doesn't know who Detective Inspector Fisher's friends are, either.'

'No, he might not.'

'I realise you're worried, Mrs Peel, but I think it's reassuring news.'

'You do?'

'Yes. He told Detective Inspector Morris that he had

some things to sort out and that he wouldn't be able to work for a while. Even though it sounds vague, it's still a reason for his absence.'

'True.'

'There's not a great deal you can do about it.'

'Frustratingly, there isn't.'

'I think he'll call on you when he's ready. Clearly something else is occupying his time at the moment.'

'You're right, Fred. You talk a lot of sense.'

He looked bashful. 'Thank you.'

'I'm going to go and buy some more bird seed,' said Augusta.

'I can go. It's my fault we've run out because I threw it all over the shop.'

'With good reason! It's fine, Fred, I'll go. And I think I may pay Mr Fairburn a visit on my way back.'

'Really?'

'If he's behind this mess, then I can't let him get away with it.'

In the shop, Saunders Animal Supplies, Augusta was served by Lucy.

'It doesn't seem long since you were last in here buying bird seed, Mrs Peel.' She weighed the seed on the scales. 'Has that canary of yours eaten it all already?'

'I wish I could blame it on Sparky. Unfortunately, the bag of bird seed had to be used as a missile to chase away some troublemakers.'

'Oh no, really? Is everything alright?'

'Just about.'

'There's not much left in the sack. I'll put the rest in the bag for you, but I won't charge you the extra.'

'There's no need—' But Lucy had already tipped it in. 'Alright, thank you.'

'I'll ask Mary to fetch another sack from the storeroom in a moment.'

'Mary?'

'She's our new girl. That will be threepence, Mrs Peel.'

Augusta thanked her again and went on her way, preparing herself for her visit to Mr Fairburn.

Webster's bookshop was a short walk from Augusta's shop in Bury Place. It was a smart street with well-presented shops and Victorian red brick apartment blocks. Webster's had fresh white paintwork and a shiny paned window. Augusta peered in through the window before entering and saw a neat, yet dull, display of Hugh Walpole's new book, *The Captives*.

Inside, the shop had a carpeted floor and a pleasant tangy smell of new paper. It was quite different from the faintly musty smell of the old books in Augusta's shop.

'Can I help you?' asked an austere young woman who looked far too youthful to be so humourless. Augusta wondered if she was Mr Fairburn's daughter.

'I'd like to speak to Mr Fairburn, please.'

'I shall find out if he's available. May I ask your name?'

'Mrs Peel.'

The young woman's face fell as she no doubt realised who she was speaking to. 'Alright.'

She disappeared into a door behind the counter and Mr Fairburn emerged a moment later with a scowl on his face. 'What do you want?'

'And good morning to you too, Mr Fairburn.'

'Good morning,' he huffed.

'I'd like you to stop targeting my shop, please.'

He gave a laugh. 'Are you accusing me of something, Mrs Peel?'

'Yes. In recent days, the landlord's agent has visited me

to relay an anonymous complaint and this morning a group of children ran in and pulled books off the shelves. Both incidents happened shortly after you visited me and accused me of stealing your customers.'

Augusta noticed the young woman's mouth drop open. She clearly hadn't been aware what Fairburn had been up to.

'Nonsense!' he responded. 'Do you honestly think I would waste my time behaving in such an infantile manner?'

'Yes.'

'Can I ask you to please leave my establishment.'

'Only when you promise me there'll be no more attacks on my shop.'

'I'm sorry to hear someone is attacking your business, Mrs Peel. Perhaps you now realise what it's like? You've been attacking my business ever since you opened your shop.'

'There are lots of bookshops in Bloomsbury, Mr Fairburn. Surely all of them pose some competition to your shop here?'

'I hadn't noticed any detrimental effect on my business until your shop opened, Mrs Peel.'

'So you are behind the attacks on my shop?'

'No!'

'If you do it again, then I will have to call the police.'

'You do that, Mrs Peel. But the police will want evidence. And what evidence do you have? Nothing.'

Augusta had an urge to knock his spectacles off his bald head. Instead, she took a breath and tried to remain calm. 'You'll regret this, Mr Fairburn.' She wasn't sure why she had said it. How was she going to make him regret what he had done?

'Oh will I? It will be interesting to see what you have in store, Mrs Peel.'

He pronounced her name with a drawn-out childish whine. Augusta turned and left, desperately trying to keep control of the anger which surged within her.

Chapter 17

MRS SAUNDERS ASKED Mary for a word in the storeroom at lunchtime. 'This is a difficult conversation to have with you, so I'll make it as quick as possible. Some money went missing from the till yesterday and the day before.'

Mary felt a cold sensation in her stomach. How could Mrs Saunders accuse her?

'It wasn't me,' she said. 'I'd never steal.'

'You seem like an honest, hard-working girl to me, Mary. And I've been extremely pleased with your work since you arrived here. But this has never happened before and it's an odd coincidence that it's happened since you began working in this shop. I realise some errors occur when handing out change to customers. Sometimes the books don't completely tally at the end of each day for that reason. But the same amount, two days in a row is unusual. We're not talking about a large amount, but it's missing all the same. Five shillings. It's an easy amount to take from a till.'

'I didn't take it, Mrs Saunders, I promise you.'

'It can only have been you or Lucy and she's been working for me for two years now with nothing like this happening.'

It had to be Lucy. Mary knew she didn't like her and she had done this because she knew Mrs Saunders would blame the new arrival.

'I promise you now, Mrs Saunders, I didn't take any money from the till.'

Her employer stood back, her arms folded. 'I'm sure you can see what a dilemma I face, Mary. Although I want to believe you, I also can't see how you can be blameless. There have only been three of us using the till over the past few days. It wasn't me and I know it wasn't Lucy.'

'Have you asked her?'

'Not yet. I shall mention it to her. But I don't see why she should start stealing from me now when she's never done it before.'

Mary wanted to tell her it was because Lucy wanted Mrs Saunders to think the new employee was a thief. But she suspected an accusation like that would antagonise Mrs Saunders. She was clearly loyal to Lucy.

For the time being, there was nothing Mary could do to change Mrs Saunders's mind. She could only hope she could keep her job. She wanted to work well and get a good reference for her next job. It would ruin her plans if she was dismissed on suspicion of stealing.

'I shall give you one more chance, Mary,' said Mrs Saunders. 'Perhaps the money went missing because of an error, I don't know. But if this happens again, then I shall have to dismiss you. In the meantime, I shall deduct the missing amount from your wages.'

'But I didn't take the money!'

Mary could tell from Mrs Saunders's expression that

this almost convinced her. But then her lips pursed and Mary felt her mind was made up.

As she emerged from the storeroom, she noticed a smirk on Lucy's face.

Mary resolved she would get her back.

Chapter 18

AUGUSTA WALKED BACK to her flat on Marchmont Street that evening, feeling despondent. It was dark now and the street lighting struggled to penetrate the cold fog which had hung over the city all day.

She regretted visiting Mr Fairburn and confronting him. She had made a threat she couldn't follow up on and it had sounded foolish. What was he going to do next? And what could she do about it? He had been right when he had said the police needed evidence. Reporting his actions was hopeless unless she could prove he was responsible.

Augusta stopped at the shop on the corner to buy some bread, then continued on her way with the loaf in one hand and Sparky's cage in the other.

A figure loitered outside the tailor's shop below her flat. Augusta paused. Was it someone waiting for her? They were little more than a silhouette in the gloom.

If it was Mr Fairburn, then she would happily tell him what she thought of him as loudly as she liked without caring who overheard.

The man leant on a walking stick. Did Mr Fairburn use a walking stick?

No. But now she recalled who did.

She strode towards the man, confident that she recognised him. But was she just being hopeful?

'Philip?' The moment she said his name, she felt sure she had been mistaken. He looked thinner. Possibly older, too.

'Augusta.'

'It *is* you!'

'Of course it is.'

She could just see his smile in the darkness.

'You're back! You're actually here!'

'Yes.' He laughed.

'I've been so worried about you.'

'Worried? Why?'

'But you're alright?'

'Yes.'

'Come on up.'

'I will. But you go ahead of me. I take some time getting up three flights of stairs with this stick.'

'Shall I put the kettle on?'

'Please do.'

A short while later, Augusta and Philip sat in her small sitting room with a cup of coffee each. Sparky fluttered between the curtain rail and the back of a dining chair.

'I'm so relieved you're back,' said Augusta. 'Where've you been?'

'I had a little holiday.'

'A holiday?' The word made her think of seaside resorts and sunshine. 'In January?'

He gave a soft laugh. 'It sounds rather odd, I realise that.'

There was something in his eyes which made him look different. Sadness maybe? And there appeared to be more lines on his face. Something had happened to him, and she wondered if he was going to be forthcoming about it. Asking him lots of questions probably wouldn't help. She sensed she would have to be patient with him.

Philip watched the canary hop up onto the edge of a lampshade. 'Has the canary been behaving himself in my absence?'

'You'll be pleased to hear that he has.'

'Good. And how's your bookshop doing?'

'Well, thank you. Perhaps a little too well.'

'What do you mean by that?'

'A bookshop owner nearby says I'm stealing his business from him. Anyway, I shan't bore you with that now. Tell me where you went on holiday.'

'The Norfolk Broads.'

Augusta had never been, but from what she had heard about the area, she pictured a flat landscape criss-crossed by calm waterways. 'Beautiful.'

'Yes, it is. I stayed with an elderly aunt.'

Augusta sipped her coffee and resisted the urge to ask why a Scotland Yard detective would take a sudden break from his work and go to stay with an elderly aunt in Norfolk. She waited for him to tell her.

A long pause followed. Philip stared ahead of him, probably hoping she would speak. Eventually, he decided to be forthcoming. 'It wasn't a scheduled holiday.'

'I can imagine not. In the middle of January.'

'Yes, it was a bit chilly.' He turned to her and smiled. Then focused his gaze ahead of him. 'The truth is… my wife has left me.'

'Oh.' Finally, she understood what he was going through. 'I'm so sorry.'

'It's been a bit of a blow. My son is with her because that makes sense, of course. But…' He rubbed his brow. 'That's why I went away and had a short holiday.'

'I can hardly imagine it was a holiday.'

'You're right, it wasn't. Anyway, my great aunt is fit and well and was pleased to see me. And my wife and son are staying with her parents in Bognor Regis.'

'I see.'

'So I've accounted for my absence.' He turned to her again. 'Does that clear up the mystery?'

'Yes it does.' She wanted to somehow comfort him without seeming improper. The best she could do was reach out and rest her hand on his arm. He pursed his lips and took a gulp of coffee.

'I returned to work today,' he said. 'And the case of Celia Hawkins is quite puzzling. I read about it in the paper when I was in Norfolk and it's a shame my colleagues have made no progress with it. Detective Inspector Petty is working on the investigation and I had a sneaky look at the file while he was taking a break for lunch today.'

'What have you found out?'

'The main suspect is a chap called Tommy Barnes. He and Celia lived together as man and wife in Battersea. He's a member of the criminal class and has served time in prison for robbery. He has an alibi for the time Celia Hawkins was murdered, but there's a possibility he's asked some friends to cover for him. Interestingly, he was arrested this morning for a violent outburst on Fleet Street.'

'What happened?'

'He appears to have caused damage to a number of shopfronts, then punched a gentleman who remonstrated with him.'

'Oh dear. I wonder why he did that?'

'I don't know. It appears to have been an angry outburst, but I don't know the reason for it.'

'Grief?'

'It's possible. Or a guilty conscience. Who knows? Another theory about Celia Hawkins's murder is that it was a robbery which went wrong. There's a female gang of thieves in Bermondsey and they've been known to target people crossing Tower Bridge at night. One of them robbed Celia Hawkins last month.'

'I read about that. And it made me wonder why she returned to the bridge at night if she'd been robbed there before.'

'It's an interesting question. Logic would suggest she would have stayed away. And that brings me onto the next puzzling point, no one seems able to explain what she was doing there. She lived and worked in Battersea. So why was she a few miles away on Tower Bridge?'

'Perhaps she was there for the same reason she was there when she was robbed last year.'

'She could have been. It's difficult when we can't be sure. Tommy Barnes has shed little light on it from what I read of the interview with him.'

'Perhaps the gang of thieves is responsible,' said Augusta. 'But why murder Celia?'

'Maybe she fought back? That's the only reason I can think of. However, the post-mortem revealed she was stabbed in the back.'

'Really?'

'It suggests her assailant approached her from behind and inflicted the wound before they'd even robbed her.'

'Or perhaps Celia was stabbed as she tried to get away?'

'In which case, why didn't the killer just let her get

away? The fact she was stabbed in the back doesn't suggest to me she was putting up a fight.'

'How horrible. Are there any other suspects?'

'Well, the gang has quite a few members, but I don't understand why a thief would become a murderer. However, I don't have a full understanding of the case yet. I'm just relying on what I managed to read of the file while Detective Inspector Petty was having his lunch. There were a few notes in the file from witness reports, and I read some of them. Someone apparently saw Celia Hawkins in the company of a smartly dressed gentleman leaving L'Épicurien restaurant in Covent Garden. The date on the note was about a week ago and I couldn't find anything in the file which suggested someone had investigated it further.'

'So you could investigate it.'

'Not really.'

'Why not? Because it's Detective Inspector Petty's case?'

'Yes. I haven't been assigned to it and it would put his nose out of joint if I got involved.'

'But he hasn't done anything!'

'He's done quite a bit, he's interviewed a lot of people.'

'But he hasn't caught the killer.'

'It's a complicated case, Augusta. And there's a possibility Petty has investigated the lead but not updated the file with his findings yet.'

'I don't think he has.'

'What makes you so sure?'

'It's just a feeling.'

Philip laughed. 'You can't just base a judgement on a feeling, Augusta.'

'Why not? It's served me well in the past. It served me well in Belgium a few times, didn't it?'

'It certainly did.'

'I think you need to investigate the lead which Detective Inspector Petty has ignored.'

'It's not the done thing, Augusta.' Then he finished his coffee and gave a smile. 'But that doesn't mean I shouldn't do it.'

Chapter 19

'THE DASHING INSPECTOR'S BACK?' said Lady Hereford. She sat in her bath chair in the middle of Augusta's shop and wore a peacock blue coat and matching hat. 'That's wonderful news! Isn't it wonderful news, Fred?'

'Yes it is, Lady Hereford.'

'All that worry for nothing, Augusta! So where's he been?'

'To the Norfolk Broads.'

'Good grief. Why?'

'He wanted to get away for a bit because his wife has left him.'

'How awful. Why did she do that?'

'I'm not entirely sure. He hasn't told me all the details. I think he's probably more upset about it than he seems.'

'I'm sure he is! The poor man. Although perhaps he had an extramarital love affair?'

'I don't think so.'

'He probably won't admit to you if he has. He's probably feeling rather ashamed about it.'

'I don't think Philip would have an affair. He doesn't seem the type at all. And besides, who with?'

'I don't know, Augusta. He's quite the mysterious type, isn't he?'

'Yes, he's mysterious, but he wouldn't do something like that to his wife and son.'

'Well, one of these days you'll need to ask him.'

'Why?'

'Because I want to know these things! I can't believe you haven't asked him already, Augusta. It would have been the first question to come out of my mouth.'

'I prefer to be tactful.'

'Yes, I realise that, and it's probably the best way to be. For some reason, I manage to get away with my directness when really I shouldn't. Perhaps he'll confess all before long. He's clearly quite upset about things, but if you ply him with whisky…'

'That's not the sort of thing I like to do either.'

'Oh Augusta! You're always so correct about everything. Just think what you could achieve if you could loosen his tongue a little.'

'His personal affairs are none of my business. We may have known each other for a long time and worked together during the war, but his marriage is his business. I just feel very sorry for him because he looks rather lost about it.'

'I expect he does. Men are always lost when their wives leave them. Perhaps Mrs Fisher will have a change of heart and return. Oh, I wish I knew what had happened between them, even though I barely know the man. I can't help being fascinated by other people's lives, it's a particular weakness of mine. Now is he working on the Tower Bridge murder case? I haven't read much about it in the papers recently and I can only assume they haven't made a great deal of progress with it.'

'One of his colleagues is working on it. And you're right, little progress has been made.'

'So you two need to be working together on it, then. You'll soon have it solved, just as you did with the other cases.'

'There was probably a bit of luck involved with those.'

'Don't talk yourself down, Augusta! It wasn't about luck at all. It was a magnificent effort from the pair of you. You work well together. I suppose it's what you did during the war, too. I think Scotland Yard is foolish if it doesn't allow the pair of you to solve this latest murder. Just think what the poor woman's family is going through! They have to wait while the Yard twiddles its thumbs and does nothing to find the killer. And someone that vicious could strike again, couldn't they?'

'I hope they don't.'

'Me neither. Can you pass me the bird seed for Sparky, please?'

Augusta did so.

'I managed to frighten away a group of urchins with bird seed yesterday,' said Fred.

'Really?'

Fred told Lady Hereford the story. 'It seems Mr Fairburn has a vendetta against us,' he added.

'Dreadful! Would you like me to speak to Sir Pritchard about it?'

'Not just yet,' said Augusta.

'Why not?'

'We don't actually have any proof that Mr Fairburn is behind this. Although we're assuming he is.'

'And I think you're assuming correctly.' She fed Sparky some more bird seed. 'And that silly agent should have known better than to believe some complaint from Mr Fairburn. It's quite obvious the bookshop owner has a vested interest in making life difficult for you. I wonder what we can do in return?'

'I don't believe in retaliation, Lady Hereford.'

'Why not? It's fun!'

'It can be never-ending. And I prefer to think that I'm better than Mr Fairburn. I don't feel the need to sink to the depths which he has.'

'A very sensible approach, Augusta. You're far more sensible than me. I think I would have gone round there by now and thrown eggs at his door.'

'Hopefully Mr Fairburn will grow bored with it and realise that my bookshop is here to stay.'

'Well, I think it might take a little more than that. But if there are any more problems, Augusta, then please let me know. I'm friends with all the right people in all the right places.'

'You're a useful person to know, Lady Hereford.'

'I am. And I'm not getting any younger. Make the most of me while I'm still here.'

Chapter 20

AFTER CLOSING the shop for the day, Augusta walked through the rain down to Covent Garden, where she had arranged to meet Philip.

She felt relieved he was back, and she was happy that he had sought her out so soon after his return. But she was also worried about him. There was little doubt he was suffering some heartache and she didn't know how she could help him.

He was already waiting for her outside L'Épicurien restaurant on Floral Street, leaning on his walking stick. He stood beneath the light of a lamppost. The raindrops around him were illuminated like hundreds of little fireflies. She fancied for a moment they were meeting for dinner, but swiftly pushed the idea from her mind. They were working together and nothing more.

'Good evening, Augusta.' He doffed his bowler hat. 'Shall we go in?'

It was still early in the evening and only a few customers were inside. Each table was covered with a white cloth and lit with a candle. A waiter bustled up to them, menus in hand. 'A table for two?'

'No, thank you,' said Philip. 'I'm Detective Inspector Fisher of Scotland Yard.' He produced his warrant card. 'And this is my colleague, Mrs Peel. Can we speak to the manager, please?'

'Of course.' The waiter gave a respectful nod. 'I shall fetch Mr Darnell for you.'

A few minutes later, Augusta and Philip sat at one of the candlelit tables with Mr Darnell. He was a slight man with black, combed-back hair and a prominent nose.

'We're looking for the murderer of this young woman,' said Philip. He showed the restaurant manager a picture of Celia Hawkins, which had been cut from a newspaper. Augusta suspected a better photograph of her was in the file in Scotland Yard, but it had to remain there for Detective Inspector Petty to use.

Mr Darnell peered at the photograph. 'I don't recognise her. Has she been in here?'

'We've had a report she was here a few weeks ago. A witness said she accompanied a well-dressed gentleman.'

'Do you know what date?'

'I'm afraid not.'

The manager sighed. 'If you don't know exactly when, then I'm going to struggle to help you.'

'I appreciate it's not very much,' said Philip. 'Sometimes it's all we get from a witness.'

'I understand. Let me ask my staff. Perhaps one of them remembers the couple.' He picked up the picture and disappeared through a door at the back of the restaurant.

'It was a good idea to come here, Augusta,' said Philip. 'Your feeling was correct. Petty can't have visited this place. If he had, then Mr Darnell would have told us so.'

'I just hope someone recognises her. There's a possibility, though, that the witness was mistaken.'

'There is. And in cases like this we can receive a lot of sightings which turn out to be nothing at all. But everything has to be followed up, no matter how tedious it may seem at times. Ah, this looks promising.'

Mr Darnell was now walking towards them with a young waitress. She had mousey brown bobbed hair and bowed her head with shyness.

'This is Miss Perkins,' said the manager. 'She thinks she recognises the lady in the picture. She doesn't know who she is but, anyway, you tell them, Katie.'

'I think she's the lady who came in here with Sir Charles,' she said. Augusta had to strain her ears to listen to her quiet voice.

'Sir Charles?' said Philip.

'Granger. The newspaper man,' said Mr Darnell. 'He's a regular visitor. He often brings friends here and the occasional lady friend, too.'

Philip turned to Miss Perkins. 'You're quite sure about this?'

She nodded.

'Did you get an idea of the relationship between them?'

'No, not really.'

'Were they affectionate with each other?'

'No, I didn't see that.'

'Any disagreement that you noticed?'

She shook her head again. 'No.'

'How did their mood seem?'

'Just normal.'

'So they were just calmly chatting and enjoying their meal, you would say?'

'Yes. That's exactly what it was like. I didn't serve them, but I know who Sir Charles is.'

'And when was this?'

'About three weeks ago.'

Augusta hoped the young woman wasn't mistaken. A waitress encountered lots of people every day. Most of them would be forgettable unless they stood out for a particular reason.

Philip seemed to think the same. 'And how sure are you that Celia Hawkins, the woman in this picture, is the same woman you saw with Sir Charles?'

'Fairly sure.'

'Can you suggest how sure that is with a score out of ten?'

'Seven.'

'That seems fair. Thank you, Miss Perkins.'

'You could ask him, Detective Inspector,' said Mr Darnell.

'Ask Sir Charles? Yes, I think we shall.'

Chapter 21

Mrs Flynn seemed agitated at breakfast. 'Have you finished, Mr Robinson?' she said to the old man in the grey cardigan. 'You can carry on reading your paper in your room. I want to clear your table.' He grumbled a little before departing. The other two lodgers had already left for the day.

Once Mr Robinson had left, Mrs Flynn positioned herself at Mary's table, her arms folded.

'My sister told me you stole from her.'

Mary gulped back a mouthful of toast and felt the lump remain in her throat as she explained. 'I didn't! I would never dream of doing such a thing!'

'I hope not. Because my sister and I have both been very good to you. We've given you bed, board and a wage. It would be an extremely ungrateful thing to do.'

'Yes, it would, and that's why I didn't do it.' She paused and took a mouthful of tea, trying to wash down the ball of toast. 'I haven't mentioned this to your sister because I know how much she likes her.'

'Likes who?'

'Lucy. She hates me. And I think she took the money to spite me.'

Mrs Flynn gave a snort. 'I know Lucy. She'd never do something like that.'

'She seemed nice when I first began working there but, for some reason, she doesn't like me. Even though I didn't take that money, I've agreed with your sister that I will work the hours to pay for it. I want to get on well there, so I'm doing the best I can.'

Mrs Flynn's face softened a little. 'I hope I can believe you, Mary, because if I can't…'

'You can. I promise.'

'Well, at the moment my sister is still convinced you took that money.'

'That's because she likes Lucy and trusts her. She doesn't know Lucy dislikes me. And Lucy only took the money to get me into trouble. I know she likes your sister a lot. I can only hope she confesses to her and returns the money. I hope her conscience gets the better of her.'

'Well, that doesn't sound like Lucy at all.'

'I realise that. It's my word against hers. I hope she'll grow to like me eventually.'

'So do I. My sister needs staff she can rely on. You do realise that if I discover you're lying to me, I shall throw you out without a moment's notice?'

'Yes, I realise that. I certainly don't take your hospitality for granted, Mrs Flynn.'

'Good. I'm choosing to believe you on this occasion because you seem to me to be telling the truth. I'm not sure that Lucy took the money, though. Perhaps it was someone else. It doesn't really make sense and perhaps I'm foolish for putting any trust in you, because I actually know very little about you.'

Mary gulped down more tea.

'I was born in London and my family moved to Bournemouth about ten years ago. I've come back to London because I miss it and there's a lot more going on here.'

'And you can find yourself a husband.'

'I'd like to do that, yes.'

Her face flushed warm, and she tried to finish her toast, even though her appetite had gone.

Chapter 22

THE SUN SHONE weakly through the clouds on Fleet Street the following morning as Augusta and Philip made their way to Sir Charles's office. Augusta had asked Fred to mind the shop for a few hours and hoped he wouldn't get any bother from Mr Fairburn while he did so.

'Sir Charles Granger owns two newspapers,' Philip said to Augusta. 'The *Evening Gazette* and the *Morning Express*. Apparently they were both good newspapers once upon a time but have declined in quality since he bought them.'

'It doesn't sound like he's very good at his job then.'

'It doesn't, does it? But I'll do my best not to judge him until I've met the man.'

'Do you have an appointment?' asked the young man who answered the door to them.

'No, because I'm a Scotland Yard detective,' replied Philip, showing him his warrant card.

'Oh.' He stepped aside and allowed Augusta and Philip to walk into the spacious, tiled hallway.

'I shall accompany you to his office,' said the young

man. 'Although he doesn't like receiving visitors unannounced.'

'I'm sure he'll be very pleased to see us,' said Philip, giving Augusta a grin.

They followed the young man up a staircase and along a corridor. They reached a polished door with the name 'Sir Charles Granger' etched on a bronze plaque.

'I shall go in first,' said the young man. 'And explain who you are. May I ask what it is you wish to speak to him about?'

'I'd prefer to tell him myself,' said Philip.

'I see. Very well.' He knocked and went into the room. They listened to the muffled voices beyond the door before he reappeared. 'Sir Charles is very busy.'

'I'm sure he is. This won't take long.'

'Alright.'

Inside Sir Charles's office, pale sunlight streamed through tall windows. A well-dressed man with a waxed moustache stood with his back to the fireplace, smoking a cigar.

Augusta recognised him immediately. He was the gentleman who had visited her shop and bought a dozen books from her.

'Well, well, well,' he said, surveying Philip. 'What have I done to deserve a visit from the Yard?' Then his eyes rested on Augusta and he smiled. 'And if it isn't the delightful lady from the bookshop!'

Philip gave Augusta a quizzical look.

'My copy of *The Hound of the Baskervilles* is just there,' he pointed his cigar at the book on a side table. 'And I'm enjoying it very much. For the second time. So what is the lady from the bookshop doing with a detective from Scotland Yard?'

'Mrs Peel and I are colleagues.'

'You're a policewoman, Mrs Peel?'

'No. I'm an investigator. I assist Detective Inspector Fisher with his cases.' This description made her seem more official than she actually was.

'How interesting, I've never heard of that before.' His jaw jutted pugnaciously. 'A bookseller, a book repairer and an investigator. You're clearly a lady of many talents. Please come and take a seat, the pair of you, and tell me how I can help you.'

They followed him to a desk at the end of the room and sat down.

'Have you heard of the murder of Celia Hawkins?' Philip asked.

'Is that the young lady who fell off the bridge?'

'Tower Bridge. Yes. And she was attacked with a knife before being pushed off. Her body was found two days later at Rotherhithe.'

'I recall hearing about it now.' He inhaled on his cigar.

'I understand you knew Miss Hawkins,' said Philip.

'Knew her?' Sir Charles raised an eyebrow.

'Did you?'

'No, I didn't.'

'Are you familiar with L'Épicurien restaurant on Floral Street in Covent Garden?'

Sir Charles hesitated a little, as if wondering whether his answer would trip him up. 'I've visited the place in the past.'

'I spoke to the manager there recently, Mr Darnell, and he told me you're a regular visitor.'

One side of Sir Charles's mouth lifted in a contemptuous smile. 'So why did you ask me if I knew the place then?'

'I wanted to confirm it with you.'

'You were testing me, trying to find out if I was going to be truthful with you.'

'Well, that is the job of a detective, I'm afraid.'

Sir Charles sat back in his chair and jabbed his cigar in Philip's direction. 'That's why I have a problem with chaps like you. You're always trying to trip people up. Always trying to be a bit clever. You're not straight talkers. I don't like people who can't talk straight and say things as they are.'

'Do you mind if we return to the topic? I understand you're a busy man.'

'Go on.'

'You never knew Celia Hawkins?'

'No.'

'And yet we have witnesses who say they saw you dining with her in L'Épicurien restaurant three weeks ago.'

'Your witnesses are mistaken, Detective Inspector Fisher. It's as simple as that.'

'Aren't you the least bit concerned about what happened to her?'

'It's very sad, yes. But I didn't know her.'

'Perhaps you can tell me who the young lady was who you were seen dining with?'

'I would, Detective Inspector, but I don't know which young lady it was. I've dined with many of them over the years. I'm sure she was delightful company, whoever she was. They always are.'

He gave a smile which left a bitter taste in Augusta's mouth. She sensed they wouldn't get much more from him, and he was clearly prepared to defend himself.

'Can I ask what you were doing on the evening of Monday the tenth of January?' Philip asked.

'I would have to ask my secretary to consult my diary.'

'Perhaps you can ask your secretary, then?'

Sir Charles scowled. 'Why are you asking me to account for my time, Detective Inspector?'

'Because it's my job, Sir Charles.'

He sighed, picked up a telephone receiver and requested that his official diary be brought into the office.

Moments later, a woman in a grey dress and wearing steel-rimmed spectacles entered the room.

'Can you tell these people what I was doing on Monday the tenth of January please, Miss Macmillan?'

The secretary leafed through the book. 'At eight o'clock you dined with the Member of Parliament for Surbiton, Mr Galsworthy.'

'Thank you. I do believe that was at Restaurant Frascati in Westminster. Can you confirm that for the detective, please?'

'That's right.'

Sir Charles turned to Philip. 'If you have any doubt about what my secretary has just told you, then I'm sure the details can be verified with both Mr Galsworthy's office and the restaurant itself.'

'Thank you,' said Philip. 'That's most helpful.' He turned to the secretary. 'Would you mind telling me what other dinner appointments Sir Charles had in the weeks preceding that date?'

She looked to her employer for confirmation, and he gave her a stiff nod.

Miss Macmillan placed the diary on the desk and Philip got out his notebook and made notes as she leafed through the pages. Sir Charles puffed on his cigar and glared at Philip.

'Thank you,' said Philip after a few minutes and put his notebook and pen away. 'And thank you for your time, Sir Charles. We won't detain you any longer.' He got up from his chair and Augusta did the same. 'If you do remember anything, you can contact me at the Yard.'

'I'm sure you have all you need.'

'I didn't realise you'd met that man before,' said Philip once they had left the office building.

'Neither did I. He visited my shop and bought a lot of books, but I didn't know his name.'

'Well, it's nice to hear you got some money out of him. So what do you think? Did he tell us the truth?'

'Of course he didn't. His claim that he dines with so many young women he can't remember them turns my stomach. If he can't remember them all, then how can he be so sure that one of them wasn't Celia Hawkins?'

'Exactly. He appears to have some convenient memory loss, doesn't he? And he wasn't the least bit interested in helping us. I think a decent chap is always ready to help with the case of a murder like this. There's concern for the victim and an urge to be as helpful as possible. We didn't see that at all and that immediately makes me think he has something to hide.'

He stopped and pulled out his notebook. 'I don't think he was happy about me writing down all his appointments, but I'm pleased I managed to do it. From what I can see, he visited L'Épicurien three times in the weeks before Celia Hawkins was murdered. All that's noted in the diary is the name of the restaurant and the time. I'm assuming his secretary booked the table for him each time. The name of the people he dined with hasn't been noted, however.'

'That could suggest he made the arrangements privately with the people he dined with.'

'It does, doesn't it? If it was something more formal, then I think it's likely the secretary would have written the names of the people he was with. She seemed to do so on some of the other entries I read.'

'So we don't know for sure that Sir Charles dined with Celia Hawkins at L'Épicurien.'

'The best evidence we have is a waitress who says she saw him with a woman who looked like Celia. So it's difficult to prove anything at this stage. But I think we can also make some judgements about the man based on his unhelpful conduct.'

They continued on their way, heading west towards the Strand. 'I think I shall hop on a bus here and head out west to Hammersmith. Would you like to accompany me or do you have to get back to your shop?'

'That depends on where you're going.'

'Wormwood Scrubs prison. It's where Celia Hawkins's common-law husband, Tommy Barnes, is being detained for a week after his outburst of anger.'

'Prison? I can't think of anywhere better to spend the morning.'

Chapter 23

SIR CHARLES MASHED his cigar into the ashtray on his desk. The last thing he needed was Scotland Yard asking him questions. Who were the witnesses who had spoken to them? Could one of them have been Piggers? He refused to believe an old friend would do such a thing, but he didn't understand how else the police knew he'd had dinner with Celia Hawkins.

And what was the lady from the bookshop up to? Her presence made little sense to him. He'd had no idea she was friendly with the police. It was a shame, because he had liked her the first time he met her.

He caught sight of the *Morning Express* on his desk and remembered why he had been in a foul temper even before the detective and the strange bookseller lady had turned up. He picked up his telephone and spoke to his secretary. 'Ask Mr Ladbroke to visit me at once, please.'

Then he sat back in his chair and thought about the detective he had just spoken to. He clearly wasn't stupid, and no doubt realised he had lied about meeting Celia Hawkins. The detective would probably find more witnesses and, before long, he was going to have to admit to it. What excuse could he come up with for having had dinner with her? He had to think of something now so he could remain one step ahead of the police.

The telephone on his desk rang and he lifted the receiver. 'Mr Ladbroke says he is tied up at the moment,' said Miss Macmillan. 'Will this afternoon at two o'clock do?'

'No. Tell him I want to see him immediately.'

'Very well, sir.'

Five minutes later, the editor of the *Morning Express*, Mr Ladbroke, sat opposite him. He had a square face and thinning hair. His expression was glum, as if he was expecting a scolding. 'Will our meeting take long, sir? I'm trying to resolve a problem with one of the reporters before finalising today's edition.'

'It will take as long as it takes,' replied Sir Charles, leafing leisurely through the morning's edition. He enjoyed prolonging the editor's discomfort. To add to it, he assumed an expression of disapproval as he perused the pages in front of him. 'I don't think this morning's edition was up to scratch,' he said eventually.

'May I ask which particular bit?'

'All of it, Ladbroke, all of it.'

'Oh.'

'In fact, I've been unimpressed with the paper for the past few weeks. You appear to be dropping the intellectual articles in favour of... police news.'

'If you're referring to the coverage of last night's robbery, sir, I'd consider that to be more than police news.'

'Would you? I disagree. Where's the commentary on the unemployment programme resolution from the Labour

Party and Trade Union Congress conference? They're suggesting forty shillings a week for every out-of-work householder. An outrageous amount!'

'There is an article on that, sir, on page seven.'

'Seven? It should be on page two or three. And it's only three hundred words long, it should be at least eight hundred.'

'We have written quite a bit about the conference, sir, and the—'

'Not enough to satisfy our readers' appetites, I'm afraid. Let's not forget who we're appealing to. Our readers are intellectuals. They want to be kept fully abreast of the important issues, not some jewellery robbery in Hatton Garden, which is not only on page one but also two, three and four.'

'A lot of jewellery was stolen, sir. I know Detective Jones of the Flying Squad quite well, and he's given me a lot of information about it.'

'So the paper is some sort of police propaganda gazette now, is it?'

'No, not at all, sir. I thought readers would be interested to read about how the heist took place. And perhaps there were witnesses which may come forward and—'

'So you're doing the job of the police now?'

'No! I thought that if we give the robbery some coverage, then perhaps members of the public could help and—'

'So you *are* doing the police's job for them. The robbery should be on page seven, Ladbroke. Page ten, even. And it requires only a hundred and fifty words. It has no relevance to the daily lives of our readers. They're interested in the matters which affect them, the events of the world. They want to know how the League of Nations is going to shape the future. Don't you think that's important after years of war and disease?'

'Yes, it is, sir—'

'Well, tell our readers all about it then! And don't feed them sensationalist stories about jewel thieves and, what was it again? That Tower Bridge murder. The problem with writing those types of stories is that it makes our readers think they can become detectives too. It's dangerous to inform them too much about such stories. Before you know it, we'll have letters from all manner of deluded people thinking they've got the answers. Have you received any?'

'Yes, we always receive a few after we've reported on a murder.'

'There you go, you see. I knew it. It's the job of the police to solve crimes, not the public.'

'But may I say, sir, that readers do like the occasional sensationalist story and it can help circulation figures.'

'Circulation figures are important, Ladbroke, I don't disagree with you there. However, they shouldn't be pursued at the expense of quality. I've given you guidelines on what I want to see covered and I'd like you to remember who our primary readers are. They're gentlemen who are keenly interested in the state of world affairs. They are the men who make the important decisions in this country. It is our job to inform them.'

'With all due respect, sir, many of those gentlemen usually take *The Times*.'

Sir Charles slammed his hand on his desk in anger. 'I don't want to hear the name of other newspapers! It's our job to provide the morning news to the great and good of this country. Do you think they want to hear about jewellery thieves? No. Now something needs to change quickly, otherwise I shall have to consider your position.'

He didn't like the way Ladbroke set his jaw. 'I am capable of considering my position myself, sir. And if you wish to make such dramatic changes to the *Morning Express*—'

'Dramatic changes?'

'I consider them dramatic, sir. I think our opinions differ too greatly for me to continue in my position, so I therefore tender my resignation with immediate effect.'

'Resign? Now?' His blood ran cold. Had he gone too far?

'I'm afraid so, sir.' Mr Ladbroke got to his feet.

'What about tomorrow morning's edition? It goes to print this afternoon!'

'Indeed it does. I suppose you'll need to find yourself a new editor by then, sir.'

Chapter 24

AUGUSTA PICKED up a copy of the *Morning Express* which someone had left on a seat on the bus. 'A jewellery robbery,' she commented, skimming her eyes over the story.

'Yes, quite a large one at a jeweller's shop in Hatton Garden,' said Philip. 'Apparently, a door was accidentally left unlocked. How do you accidentally leave a door unlocked in a shop filled with valuable jewellery? There's something suspicious about that, if you ask me.'

'You think a member of staff purposefully did it to help the robbers gain access?'

'It seems so, doesn't it? Usually, those shop owners are extremely careful about security. The Flying Squad are busy working on it.'

'The Flying Squad?'

'It's a relatively new department which investigates robberies and thefts. And for this case, they're having to draft in extra men to help them.'

Wormwood Scrubs prison was an austere brown brick

building tucked behind high walls. Its gatehouse was attractive yet forbidding, with two large hexagonal towers of brown and white stone.

'I've got no problem with you, Detective Inspector,' said the prison officer at the gate. 'But this isn't the sort of place for ladies.' He gave Augusta a sidelong glance.

'I've already explained to you that Mrs Peel is an investigator who's assisting the Yard with a serious case,' said Philip. 'I can assure you now that any unpleasantness in this place is nothing when compared to her experiences in Belgium during the war. We worked together for British intelligence there.'

Philip rarely told people this, but it had the desired effect. The officer's eyebrows raised up to the peak of his cap. 'Is that so? In which case, it shouldn't be a problem.' He turned to Augusta. 'Just be aware, madam, that it doesn't smell too good inside.'

The officer was right, the air smelt bad. Augusta and Philip followed the officer through a succession of gates. As each one slammed behind them, Augusta felt an increasing sense of claustrophobia. The jangle of keys and distant shouts echoed in her ears. This was a cold, comfortless place, and she could imagine no greater punishment than the removal of personal liberty.

The officer showed them into a room with a table, a tiny window and whitewashed walls. He left again, telling them he would fetch Tommy Barnes. The door was closed on them.

'I like to bring you to all the best places, don't I, Augusta?' said Philip.

'You do indeed. Where will you take me next?'

'Wandsworth prison perhaps? Or Brixton. That's one of my particular favourites.'

Tommy Barnes was brought into the room by two prison officers, his wrists handcuffed. He was small and lean with narrow eyes, sharp cheekbones and a thin, hardened mouth. The officers steered him to a chair opposite Augusta and Philip.

'I don't know why you coppers can't leave me alone,' he said. 'I'm already in jail. What more do you want from me?'

'Just a conversation,' said Philip. 'I'd like to speak to you about Celia Hawkins.'

'I didn't do it.' Barnes turned to Augusta. 'Who's she?'

'I'm Mrs Peel,' she replied. 'I'm helping Detective Inspector Fisher with his investigation.'

'Why?'

'It's my job to ask the questions,' said Philip. 'How long are you in here for?'

'What's it to you?'

'I'm just interested.'

'I don't see why. I'm out again soon. Now, what do you want to talk to me about? I've already told you lot all I know about Celia.'

'I realise that. But we still need more information and I'm hoping you can help us. Do you know what she was doing on Tower Bridge that night?'

'No. The only reason she went over that way was to visit St John's church in Bermondsey. But she didn't tell me she was planning on doing that. She told me she was visiting her friend Molly.'

'Do you know where Molly lives?'

'Battersea, just five minutes from where we lived. Nowhere near the bridge. So she lied to me about where she was going and I don't understand why.'

'Where can we find Molly?' asked Augusta.

'She works at Furnival Fashions. That's where Celia worked.'

'What about the night Celia was robbed on the bridge?' asked Philip. 'Where had she been going then?'

'She was visiting the church because it was the anniversary of her mother's death. I've told you lot this already. On that night, she crossed the bridge to see me in Old Jewry police station. Anyway, they took her money and her mother's wedding ring. It weren't even worth much money, but it had sentimental value. She was very upset about it.'

'Do you think she went back to the bridge that night looking for the person who stole the ring?'

'Why would she do that?'

'Perhaps she wanted to get it back?'

'If she'd wanted to do that, then she'd have taken me with her. But even she would have known there would have been no point in going back to get it because thieves always fence the stuff they take. They sell it on. As soon as you've got hold of something, you want to get rid of it as quickly as possible. And I should know.' He gave a grin.

'So you don't think her last visit to the bridge had anything to do with the fact she'd been robbed there?' asked Philip.

'I don't think so. I don't think it was revenge, even though she was angry at the robber. She told the police at Old Jewry and they did nothing about it. She also told them in Bermondsey. They know who the gangs are in that area and they know who's robbing people, but they do nothing about it. It wasn't nice when she was robbed, she was worked up about it for weeks after. But there was nothing more what could be done about it. I wanted to go down there and sort them out for myself! But the problem with gangs like that is there's always someone else higher up. And if you go there making trouble, then someone's going to make you pay for it.'

'So in summary,' said Augusta. 'Celia told you she was visiting her friend Molly that evening, but instead she went to Bermondsey to possibly visit the church.'

'That's right.' He shook his head. 'I don't understand why she kept it a secret. Why was it a secret? She must have been keeping something from me.'

'Such as what?'

'I don't know, do I? But if she was keeping a secret, then maybe it had something to do with another man. Perhaps she arranged to meet him there. I don't know why they would meet on a bridge when it's raining and blowing a gale. Seems a stupid idea to me.'

'So that's your theory?' asked Philip. 'Celia arranged to meet someone? And because she was being secretive about it, you suspect it may have been another man? A love affair, perhaps?'

Tommy scowled. 'I don't like to think of it, but that's the only reason I can think of why she didn't tell me the truth. If only she'd told me what she was doing, I would've been able to protect her. And if she did meet another man, then he's probably the one what did this to her.'

'Did Celia mention anything to you about Sir Charles Granger?' Philip asked.

Tommy's face paled, and Augusta watched him intently. Clearly, the name meant something to him. 'No,' he replied eventually. 'What about him?'

'We think Celia had dinner with Sir Charles,' said Philip.

'Where? When?'

'At L'Épicurien restaurant in Covent Garden, a few weeks before she died. Did she mention to you she'd visited the restaurant?'

'No!' His mouth hung open indignantly. 'She never mentioned nothing about it to me! How do you know about it?'

'A couple of witnesses claim to have seen them together. Have you ever heard of Sir Charles Granger?'

'No,' he said. 'I've no idea who he is.'

'So you don't know why Celia would have met with him?'

'No. Them witnesses are probably mistaken. She would've mentioned it to me.'

'But would she? She didn't tell you she was going to Bermondsey on the night she died, did she?'

'No, but…' He trailed off and his mouth twisted into a sneer.

'Perhaps she had arranged to meet Sir Charles that night?'

'Why?'

'I don't know, I'm afraid.'

'Well, I need you to find out!'

Chapter 25

Mrs Saunders had to go out to a meeting with a supplier one afternoon. 'I'll be back shortly before closing time,' she said.

Once she had left, Mary realised she had her chance to confront Lucy. The shop was quiet and Lucy stood behind the counter, filing her nails. Mary picked up a broom and began sweeping the floor. With each brush stroke, she got closer to Lucy and eventually knocked her feet.

'Ouch, do you mind?'

'It didn't hurt,' said Mary calmly.

Lucy took a step back, clearly uncomfortable with how close Mary was standing to her. 'Whether it hurt or not, it was still careless of you,' she said.

'And it was careless of you to take money from the till, hoping I'd be blamed for it.'

'What? You're accusing me of stealing?'

'Yes, I am.' Mary stepped closer to her. 'I know you took that money to get me into trouble. Mrs Saunders would never believe you took it, which is why she blamed the new girl.'

'I can't believe what you're accusing me of!'

'Neither can I. I hope you return that money to Mrs Saunders because she thinks a lot of you. She likes and trusts you.'

'And you're envious of that.'

Mary laughed. 'I'm not envious at all. But I don't like being framed for something I didn't do. So now you need to tell Mrs Saunders what really happened.'

Lucy laughed, and Mary felt a twinge of anger. She couldn't help her reaction. She shoved the broom handle across Lucy's chest and pushed her against the shelving. Then she brought her face in close and lowered her voice to a calm but threatening tone. 'Do as I say, otherwise there'll be trouble.'

Lucy's eyes were wide and frightened, but she couldn't resist answering back. 'What sort of trouble?'

'You don't want to find out.'

Mary gave Lucy another shove for good measure, then dropped the broom onto the floor. She prepared herself for a response from Lucy, but there was nothing. She hoped now she had done enough.

'I'll leave you to finish sweeping,' she said, heading for the storeroom.

Chapter 26

Augusta thought over the conversations with Sir Charles Granger and Tommy Barnes as she ate bread and vegetable soup in her flat that evening.

'Strangely, I liked Tommy Barnes more than I liked Sir Charles,' she said to Sparky. He perched on the back of the sofa. 'And yet Tommy's a thief and Sir Charles is a respected newspaper owner. Odd, isn't it?'

Sparky cocked his head, then flew up to the curtain rail.

'I don't think Tommy's a good person though,' she continued as she mopped up the remains of her soup with a piece of bread. 'I think it's possible he could have murdered Celia and is lying about the events of that evening. Would she really have gone to Tower Bridge without telling him? Was it something she was in the habit of doing? That said, I think he genuinely didn't know she'd met with Sir Charles. That news came as a shock to him, I think.'

A knock sounded at the door, and Augusta got up from

her seat and peered through the peephole. Philip gave a wave from the other side.

'Has there been a development?' she asked as she opened the door.

'There has.' He walked in, leaning on his stick.

'A good one?'

'No, not really.' He sat on the sofa and greeted Sparky on the curtain rail. Then he added, 'I've received a telling off from the commissioner.'

'Why?'

'For getting involved in a case which isn't mine to investigate.'

'No!'

'I'm afraid so. It's my own fault. Didn't I say it's not the done thing to get involved in someone else's case? I thought I should mention to Petty that I'd spoken to Sir Charles and Tommy Barnes and he reported me to the commissioner.'

'Why did you tell him?'

'Because I thought he might appreciate some help with the case. And it would have been underhand to work on it without telling him.'

'You're too sensible for your own good, Philip.'

'I don't know about that. Anyway, he didn't view my involvement as help and decided I was undermining his authority instead.'

'How ridiculous. Can't he see you can get the case solved quicker if you work together? And you were also following up a lead, which he'd ignored. How else would anyone have found out Sir Charles was known to the victim? Did you tell the commissioner that?'

'Yes, I did. But the commissioner is more interested in ensuring the rules are followed. He doesn't concern himself with the little details.'

'Well, he should! Presumably he was a detective once?'

'Indeed, he was. But the Yard is… what the Yard is. I knew at the time that I was stepping on Petty's toes. And it's all your fault, Augusta, you encouraged me to do it.'

She was about to argue when she saw the mischievous glint in his eye.

'You would have done it anyway,' she said with a smile.

'You're right, I would have done. I can't abide a shoddy job being done. And that's why Celia Hawkins's killer hasn't been caught yet. The investigation has been shoddy. But who am I to complain? I'm just a humble detective inspector.'

'So what happens now?'

'I've been told to assist the Flying Squad with the investigation of the Hatton Garden robbery.'

'So you can't work on the Celia Hawkins case at all?'

'No. Petty is working on it.'

'But he's not going to get anywhere with it!'

'Maybe he will? We can't make assumptions. Anyway, I will tell Petty how helpful you've been and you can assist him if you like. Although he's a bit of a traditionalist and may not accept your help.'

'I can't imagine him being interested in me helping him. I suppose we should just leave him to get on with it, frustrating though it is.'

'It's frustrating indeed. I certainly think Sir Charles has something to hide. And there are many more people to consider, but… we've done our best. Unfortunately, we're not free to do exactly as we please.'

He gave a sigh. He looked tired.

'Are you alright?' Augusta asked.

'Yes. Why wouldn't I be?'

'I mean with… what's happened. Your family.'

'Ah yes. Well, I prefer not to think too much about that when I'm working. It can be quite distracting.'

'But you're not working now. Surely you think about it in the evenings?'

'Not if I can help it. I keep myself busy, that's the answer.' He checked his watch. 'I should be on my way. I've got to get back to Willesden.'

'Would you like a coffee?'

'Not this evening, thank you Augusta. I'll get going. The trains have been playing up recently, so I expect I'll get delayed as it is.'

He had cut the conversation short as soon as Augusta had mentioned his wife and family. It had been a mistake to talk about them.

The following morning, Augusta travelled by train, then tram to Battersea. Scotland Yard had rules, and that was why Philip could no longer work on the Tower Bridge murder case. But the rules didn't apply to Augusta, and she doubted that Detective Inspector Petty would follow up on all the leads she and Philip had come across.

Although she didn't know the full facts of the case, Augusta felt she knew enough to continue looking into it. And having begun, she was reluctant to walk away and have nothing more to do with it.

She got off the tram on Lavender Hill and found the shop Furnival's Fashions. Mannequins stood in the window modelling fashionable low-waisted dresses in a rainbow of colours. She pushed open the door, which triggered a tinkling bell.

'Can I help you?' asked a woman with dark hair cut into a sleek, stylish bob. She wore a mauve dress similar to the style of the ones in the window.

'I'm looking for Molly,' said Augusta.

'That's me.'

'I'm Mrs Peel, I'm an investigator. I'd like to speak to you about Celia Hawkins.'

'Oh.' Her face fell.

'Is now a good time to talk?'

She glanced around the shop and bit her lip as she thought. 'We're fairly quiet at the moment, so I suppose… not here, though. How about the cafe over the road?'

'That's fine with me.'

'Can you mind things here, Joanne?' Molly called to the back of the shop. 'I'm going out for ten minutes.'

In the cafe, they ordered tea and sat by the window. 'There's more of that sleet stuff coming down,' said Molly, puffing on a cigarette. 'It might snow soon.'

'I like London in the snow,' said Augusta. 'But only for a day or two before it all goes a dirty grey colour.' She took a sip of tea. 'How well did you know Celia?'

'We were good friends once.'

'Once?'

'She couldn't be trusted. Which was a shame.'

'What did she do?'

'She stole things. I suppose it was to be expected because she was with that Tommy Barnes. She kept telling me she was trying to get him to change his ways, but she was just as bad.'

'What did she steal?'

Molly lowered her voice and leant in closer. 'I caught her stealing some scarves from the shop. We fell out over it. Although, I didn't tell Mrs Grey about it.'

'Mrs Grey?'

'She's the manageress. I didn't tell her about it because I wanted to give Celia a chance to mend her ways. It turned out she sold the scarves, but I said if she repaid the money then we could buy new stock and Mrs Grey need never know about it. I was angry with her and I don't know why I gave her another chance. I suppose I felt sorry for her.'

'Why?'

'I don't know why. She was young, twenty-four. And she hadn't always had it easy, I felt sorry for her being with that man. She tried to leave him, but he wouldn't let her. I think she was scared of him. If he said she had to be home at a certain time, then she would make sure she was there. He stayed out late a lot and on those days, it didn't matter. But if he was at home, then she had to get back as soon as she'd finished for the day. And then, occasionally, she'd have a bruise on her face and she'd say she'd knocked into something. She managed to leave him once.'

'Where did she go?'

'A friend's house, I forget who. But Tommy found her again and made her go home with him. I think she loved him. She wanted them to have a nice, respectable life together. She once told me that if he got a proper job, then he would be kinder to her. He kept promising her he would get a proper job and earn an honest living, but it never happened. She thought the people he spent time with were a bad influence on him. I think she was right about that, but he would never have changed his ways even if he had got a proper job. The best place for him is prison.'

'When did you last see Celia?'

'On the day she died. She left the shop at half-past five and then… she didn't turn up for work the next morning. Normally I would have thought that was strange, but that day I thought she was avoiding me because of something that happened the day before.'

'What happened?'

'I noticed some dresses were missing. I confronted Celia, and she denied it but I knew it was her. I told her I had no choice but to tell Mrs Grey about it. She begged me not to, but I'd already given her enough chances. So I told Mrs Grey, and I wasn't worried about her when she didn't turn up to work the next day. I thought she'd just left the shop for good. I was angry with her about it. Then, in the afternoon, Tommy Barnes came in looking for her. And when I heard she hadn't arrived home the previous night… well, we were all worried then. She'd told Tommy she was meeting me that evening, but it wasn't true.

Despite the stealing, I was really worried about her when she went missing. Then the news came she'd been found in the river.' She wiped her eyes. 'I couldn't believe it. And I still can't.'

'Have you any idea why she was on Tower Bridge that night?'

'No idea. And because she lied to Tommy about where she was going, she must have arranged to meet someone.'

'At the moment, we have only Tommy's word that she told him she was seeing you that evening.'

Molly stared at her for a moment as this thought sunk in. 'So you think he could be lying about that?'

'I don't know, but it's possible. If he did have something to do with Celia's death, then it makes sense he would lie about that evening, doesn't it?'

'Yeah.'

'How well do you know Tommy?'

'Not well at all. I only saw him a few times, but I heard a lot about him and I didn't like what I heard. He was a criminal, and he was mean to her. The more I think about it, the more I think Tommy could have done it. When he came into the shop looking for Celia, the day after she died, he had a black eye. He told us he'd been in a fight. But maybe Celia did it when she was defending herself? Perhaps she tried to leave him again and this time he wouldn't let her? He didn't deserve her and so he bullied her and made her afraid of him.'

'Why do you think Celia went back to Tower Bridge after someone robbed her there?'

'I don't know. But I know you wouldn't have caught me doing something like that. I'd have been too scared. She was upset about that robbery, she'd lost her mother's ring.'

'Do you think she could have returned to the bridge to seek revenge on the person who stole it from her?'

'I can imagine her seeking revenge, but I think she would've taken someone with her. She wouldn't have gone alone.'

Chapter 27

Tommy marched along Fleet Street with determination in his step. He had woken up that morning in a prison cell, but now he was a free man. And the first person he wanted to see was the boss.

'What are you doing here?' asked Sir Charles. Tommy had pushed past his posh assistant and charged up the stairs to Sir Charles's office.

'What were you doing with Celia?' He stood in the centre of the room and glared at Sir Charles, who reclined in his chair behind his desk.

'I beg your pardon?'

'A copper from Scotland Yard told me you had dinner with her.'

'The detective you mention has been making a nuisance of himself. Has he been pestering you too?'

'He asked me about Celia. He wants to find out who killed her. I didn't mind him because he didn't suggest it was me who did it.'

'Well, that's something to be pleased about.'

'So, did you have dinner with her? At some restaurant

in Covent Garden with a fancy French name?'

'I told the detective I had no idea who she was and that I'd never met her.'

'So why are they saying you had dinner?'

'Sit down, Tommy.'

'Not until you tell me what's been going on.'

Sir Charles rolled his eyes. 'I will explain, Tommy. Just please sit down.'

Tommy did so, keeping his eyes on Sir Charles.

Sir Charles lowered his voice. 'I did have dinner with Celia—'

Tommy's chest filled with rage. 'You what?'

Sir Charles held up a hand to pacify him. 'And it wasn't what you're thinking, Tommy. She came to see me and requested a meeting.'

'Why?'

'Because she was worried about you. She told me she'd been trying to persuade you to find a proper job and make an honest living.'

Tommy felt the anger seeping from him. It was exactly what Celia had said to him. She had told him she didn't want to be a criminal's wife. Not that they were married. But she had hoped they could get married once he became an honest man.

'I must admit I found her approach quite alarming,' said Sir Charles. 'Because no one is supposed to know you were working for me.'

Tommy sighed. 'I mentioned it to her once.'

'Why?'

'I don't know. I trusted her. I knew she wouldn't say nothing to no one. And she never did!'

'Apart from me.'

'Yeah, but she would never have told no one else.'

'I hope not. I was careful when she first spoke to me

and I initially denied knowing you. But when I realised she just wanted me to persuade you to stop what you were doing, I realised her intentions were genuine. I reminded her not to tell anyone else about my connection to you, and she agreed.'

'Celia would have kept her word,' said Tommy. But would she? He didn't know who to trust. And he still couldn't be sure that Sir Charles was telling him the truth.

'Anyway, I told Celia I would speak to you,' said Sir Charles. 'But I was terribly busy, and I didn't find the chance. And besides, it wasn't something I was quick to do.'

'Why not?'

'Because you'd stepped into Billy's shoes and you were doing a good job of running things.'

'Was I?'

'Yes.'

This flattered Tommy.

'So despite my promise to your dear Celia, letting you go wasn't something I wished to do. It was selfish of me, I realise that. But I didn't want to lose you. So that accounts for my delay in telling you about this.'

Sir Charles had flattered him, so perhaps there was some possibility of rejoining the gang. Tommy straightened his tie and slipped from his confrontational mood into subservience. 'Well, thank you for clearing that up, Sir Charles. I thought for a moment that…'

'I was conducting a love affair with her? Yes, I expect you did. I may be many things, Tommy, but I'm not a philanderer.'

'I'm sorry if I came in here angry.'

'You were given information which made you angry. It's understandable.'

'Well, now we've cleared it all up, maybe I can come back?'

He didn't like the glum expression on Sir Charles's face.

'I'm afraid little has changed since our last meeting, Tommy.'

'I'd say it has! The police don't suspect me no more.'

'How do you know that?'

'They've not arrested me and I'm quite sure there's no one following me about.'

'But you've just served some time in prison.'

'It wasn't long. And I've done time in prison plenty of times before.'

'I don't think you quite understand, Tommy. I can't be associating with a man who's a murder suspect and has just been in prison.'

'No one knows you're associating with me!'

'You're here now in my office! The detective from the Yard came here asking me questions, too. I have to be exceptionally careful at the moment. I don't think you understand what it's like for a man in my position.'

A position superior to Tommy. The condescending phrase angered him.

'But you just told me yourself that you consider me a good worker. When Celia asked you to drop me, you didn't want to! I'm good at this!'

'A lot has changed since I spoke to Celia. And besides, Frank pulled off the job in Hatton Garden quite satisfactorily.'

The words felt like a punch to Tommy's chest. He was no longer needed.

His hands balled into fists. If he stayed here a moment longer, he would lose control. He got to his feet and left.

Chapter 28

AUGUSTA'S HEART sank as she arrived at the shop the following morning to find Fred washing red paint off the paned bow window.

'Let me help,' she said.

'It's alright, I've nearly finished. Luckily, the weather was too wet overnight for it to dry.'

'This is Fairburn again?'

'It must be.'

'When is he going to give up?'

'We can report this to the police.'

'We can, but we need evidence it was he who did it. You and I know it is, but the police will want us to prove it.'

'And he wouldn't have done it himself, he'd have asked someone else to do it for him.' He dipped the rag into the bucket of water and rinsed it. Then he used the pink-tinged rag to mop off more of the paint.

'I think you're right. And if he's assuming I'm going to close my business just because he's thrown some paint at my windows, then he's a foolish man indeed.'

'You go inside and keep warm, Mrs Peel,' said Fred. 'I'm nearly finished now.'

'Alright, then. Thank you, Fred. I'll make us some nice hot tea.'

Augusta went into the shop and placed Sparky's cage on the counter. Anger filled her chest and tears pricked her eyes.

She was tired of Fairburn's bullying ways. How was she going to make him stop?

Fred had finished cleaning up the paint by the time Augusta had made the tea.

'I was having a think just then,' he said as she handed him his cup. 'I was thinking about the time when Mr Fairburn took over Webster's and told me I was dismissed.'

'Oh no. You need to push that awful man from your mind.'

'But wait, Mrs Peel. I think you'll want to listen to this.'

'Go on then.' She took a sip of tea.

'I remember I walked home sadly and wondered where I could find another job as enjoyable as Webster's. And while I was busy feeling sorry for myself, I realised I'd forgotten to hand a set of keys back to Mr Fairburn. Mr Webster had entrusted me with the keys to open and close the shop and I realised, by rights, they belonged to Mr Fairburn. After the way he'd treated me, however, I wasn't in a hurry to return them. In fact, I never did.'

Augusta felt a smile grow across her face. 'You still have them?'

He grinned. 'Yes, I have.'

'So we could visit Webster's when everyone's left for the evening and look for empty pots of red paint? I suppose Fairburn could have ensured they were thrown away, but if we can find some evidence that he's behind the recent trouble, then that would be wonderful. Shall we visit his shop this evening?'

'Yes. From what I recall, the shop is empty and locked up by half-past six. But to be on the safe side, I don't think we should visit until after eight. Just in case someone has stayed behind to do a stock take or something similar.'

'Good plan. Let's meet here at eight tonight.'

Chapter 29

TOMMY STOOD outside the tall gates of New Scotland Yard. He looked up at the imposing building and tried to ignore the anxiety in his stomach. He had spent most of his life trying to avoid the police, so what was he doing here? It went against his instincts.

But Tommy had learned that smashing up shopfronts and punching people didn't solve his problems. That was why he had left Sir Charles's office in such a hurry. He couldn't risk losing his temper again. What was that saying about revenge being a dish best served cold? He had heard it a few times and now he understood its meaning. He was giving himself a bit of time to think with clarity. It was no use reacting when his mind was clouded with fury.

He felt impressed by how quickly he had managed to calm himself. Sir Charles thought he was the powerful one, but he was mistaken. Knowledge was more powerful than money. And Tommy intended to use his knowledge as a weapon. Sir Charles had no control over him now. No one did. And he could speak to whom he liked.

He gave a shudder as he stepped into the wood-panelled reception area. He was half-expecting someone to grip his collar and march him off to a cell. To his shame, he could feel himself trembling a little. He tentatively approached the desk and spoke to the duty sergeant there.

'I want to talk to the detective with the walking stick. I can't remember his name.'

'Detective Inspector Fisher?'

'Might be. Like I say, I can't remember his name.'

'Wait here, please.'

Tommy stood with his cap in his hands, shifting from one foot to the other. He felt extremely out of place here. A man walked down the stairs and gave him a glance which seemed accusatory. Tommy looked away, keen to get his visit over and done with.

Detective Inspector Fisher appeared on the staircase a short while later. Tommy watched him descend the stairs. He did a good job of it considering he was reliant on a walking stick.

To his surprise, the detective smiled when he saw him. 'Mr Barnes! How are you?'

'I'm doing alright.'

'You're out of prison now, I see. Are you going to stay out?'

'I'll do my best.'

'How can I help?'

'I need to talk to you about something in private.'

'I see. Well, let's see if there's a room free. Follow me.'

Tommy walked behind the detective, who moved at a pace a little slower than he would have liked.

A few minutes later, they sat in a room with dark wallpaper and portraits of stern-looking senior police officers on the wall. He felt like they were all watching him.

Detective Inspector Fisher opened his notebook. As police officers went, Tommy didn't mind him too much.

Although he was a serious man, there was a softness in his eyes which hinted at a kind nature.

He cleared his throat and began. 'I've got something to tell you.'

'Very well.'

Tommy opened his mouth, but no further words came out. Was his voice failing him because he was making a big mistake? He took a breath and appreciated the fact Fisher wasn't hurrying him. Instead, he waited patiently.

He closed his eyes for a moment and thought of Celia having dinner with Sir Charles. Had Sir Charles lied to him about the true reason for their meeting? And he thought now of the anger he had felt when Sir Charles had removed him from the gang. And he was never to be allowed back again. Sir Charles had taken everything away from him.

Sir Charles was rich and powerful and people respected him. They wouldn't respect him if they knew what he was really like!

He took a breath and tried again. 'I know who's behind the Hatton Garden robbery.'

Fisher raised an eyebrow. 'You do?'

'Yeah.'

'And why are you telling me this?'

'Because of what they done to me.'

'I see. Well, if the information you're about to tell me is helpful in the investigation, then I will need to share it with my colleagues. Is that alright?'

'Yeah.'

'And if the information leads to a trial, then you may be required to appear in court—'

'Court? I'm not standing up in court!'

'You may not be required to do so. And that's only if the people you're about to mention end up standing trial. I should think we're a long way off that, yet. But before we even begin, Mr Barnes, I'd like to commend you for stepping into this place and asking to speak with me. That can't have been easy to do.'

Tommy hadn't heard a copper talk like this before, it quite impressed him. 'It weren't easy,' he said.

'And you should take comfort in the fact you're doing the right thing now.'

'I hope it's the right thing.'

'So what do you know about the Hatton Garden robbery?'

'Well, I was supposed to be in charge of it.'

'You were?'

'Yeah. For years I worked with my friend Billy Goldman and, when he got locked away, I was asked to organise the Hatton Garden job.'

'By who?'

'Sir Charles Granger.'

Fisher sat back in his chair as if he'd just been slapped in the face. '*The* Sir Charles Granger? The newspaper owner?'

'Yeah. I've visited him at his office on Fleet Street.'

Fisher scratched at his temple and leant forward again. 'You do realise this is a serious accusation, Mr Barnes?'

'Yeah.'

'And you're absolutely sure about it?'

'As sure as I'll ever be.'

'Very well. When did you last see him?'

'Today. I visited him this morning and asked him if it was true he'd had dinner with Celia.'

'And what did he say?'

'He told me it was true, and she'd called on him to ask that he dismiss me from the gang. She didn't like the work I did, you see. She wanted me to stop it. And she knew he was in charge.'

'How did she know that?'

'I told her. It was a mistake. I was bad with the drink at the time. She told no one, I'm sure of it. When I first found out he was in charge, I couldn't believe it. An important man like him who knows all the politicians and the rest of them. No one knows what he gets up to!'

'So Celia had dinner with him to ask him to remove you from the gang?'

'Yeah. Well, that's what he told me. I still don't know whether to believe him. No one can ever believe what he says.'

'Does it sound like the sort of thing Celia would have done?'

'Yeah, I can imagine her doing that.'

'Alright.' Fisher made some notes. 'What else did you speak to him about today?'

'He told me he was happy with how the job in Hatton Garden had gone and that he didn't need me no more.'

'Is that the reason you're here today?'

'Yeah. I've been with those people for over twenty years. They're all I've ever known. I grew up with them. And for most of that time, I never knew everyone answered to him. But he suddenly decides he doesn't want me involved no more. I've lost my livelihood. I realise it wasn't a legal livelihood, but I've lost it all the same. I didn't know how to earn money the ordinary way.'

'So who took over from you in organising the Hatton Garden job?'

'Frank Harrison. And Jim Fardon was involved too.' Tommy went on to give Fisher the names of all the men in the gang. Men he had grown up with and considered friends. But where had they been when he had been kicked out? No one had turned up on his doorstep to ask how he was. They had left him out in the cold. And now he was having his revenge.

'Most of them are like me and have been arrested before,' he said to Fisher. 'If you haven't heard of them before, I'm sure a lot of your colleagues will have.'

'I'm sure they will.'

'So what happens now?'

'I'll pass this information onto my colleagues and we'll get everyone rounded up.'

'Including Sir Charles?'

'He'll probably be the one we bring in last. For someone like him, we need as much evidence as possible, so we'll speak to the others to begin with. Thank you for coming to see me today, Mr Barnes. You've been extremely helpful.'

Chapter 30

Augusta arrived at her shop at eight o'clock that evening. Fred was already there, waiting in the dark doorway.

'Unfortunately, the moon is bright tonight,' he said. 'There's no cloud cover at all.'

'That explains why it's particularly cold,' said Augusta, shivering in her thick coat. 'But hopefully there are few people about tonight to notice us. What's the plan for getting into Webster's?'

'There's a back entrance which we can access from Galen's Yard behind the shop.'

'Perfect. Shall we go?'

Augusta felt a twist of nerves in her stomach as they walked to the corner of Bury Place, then turned left and left again into Galen's Yard. She was pleased to see there was only one lamppost in the yard. The rest of it was in darkness.

'I've brought my torch,' she whispered to Fred. 'Just lead the way.'

'We have to go down an alleyway to get to the door.'

Augusta could just about see Fred in the darkness. She

followed him, putting out her hand to guide her way along the rough wall. A damp, pungent odour hit her nose and turned her stomach.

'Who's there?' called out a voice from the darkness. Augusta startled and suppressed a yelp.

'We've come to check on our shop,' replied Fred, he sounded surprisingly calm.

'That's right,' said Augusta. She flicked on her torch.

'Ouch! Get that light out of my face!' said an old man sitting in the alleyway with a filthy blanket over his knees.

'I'm sorry,' said Augusta. 'And we apologise for disturbing you.'

The old man grunted. 'I can forgive all for a few shillings.'

Augusta pulled her purse out of her coat pocket and found some. 'And we'd appreciate it if you don't mention our visit here to anyone. We're planning a surprise.'

The old man gave a hearty chuckle. 'Burglars are you?'

'Do we look like burglars?'

'They come in all shapes and sizes.'

'I suppose they do,' said Augusta, keen to be on her way. 'Let's keep going.'

Fred stopped at a door a few yards on from where the old man sat. He tried his key in the lock, and, to Augusta's relief, the door opened. Her heart thudded as they stepped inside.

'This is the storeroom,' whispered Fred, closing the door behind them. 'Everything's in complete darkness, which is good. Just be careful with your torch when we're in the shop because someone might see it from the street.'

'Alright.' The torch's beam bounced off shelves of crates and boxes.

'It's not as tidy in here as it used to be,' said Fred. 'What a shame.'

Some books were unboxed and lay about on the shelves covered in a thin layer of dust.

'So what are we looking for?' said Fred. 'Paint pots?'

'Yes. And, if it exists, correspondence between Mr Fairburn and the agent. I'd like to get some evidence that he complained to them. Where's Mr Fairburn's office?'

'Upstairs. There's a doorway to the staircase in the shop.'

Fred unlocked the next door, which brought them out behind the counter. Augusta switched off her torch, as Fred had suggested. Fortunately, moonlight streamed through the shop window and there was some light to see by. Fred walked over to the door between the bookcases and opened it. Augusta couldn't see what lay beyond.

'This is a steep staircase,' he said. 'Just follow where I go.'

Augusta followed the sound of his footsteps creaking on the timber stairs and they ended up on a small landing lit by a little window.

Fred fitted a key into another door and opened it. 'Here's the office,' he whispered. 'We can probably put the torch on, but obviously we need to be careful.'

Augusta switched it on but covered part of the bulb with her palm. 'Will this do?'

'I think so. Hopefully, no one can see it.'

'There's the desk,' she said, shining the beam on it.

'An enormous desk. Much bigger than the one Mr Webster had.' It had a leather top and ornate wood panelling.

They tried opening the drawers in the desk. 'They're locked,' said Fred. 'And I don't have the keys for these.'

Augusta looked through the papers on the desktop, but she couldn't see any correspondence with the agent. They searched a cupboard and a small cabinet, but still there was nothing.

Augusta felt frustrated. 'Perhaps he's hidden or destroyed anything which could incriminate him.'

Fred didn't reply. Instead, he stood still in the centre of the room. 'I heard something,' he said.

'What?' Augusta turned her torch off and held her breath, straining her ears to listen.

The unmistakable sound of footsteps came from below.

Fred whispered a curse word. Augusta felt a cold chill run through her. 'Someone's in here?' she hissed. 'Will they come up here?'

'How do I know? We should hide.'

'Where?'

'Under Fairburn's desk,' he said. 'But move carefully, the floorboards might creak.'

Augusta's mouth felt dry as she crept carefully to the desk. As she slid beneath it, she felt sure the person downstairs had heard her move.

Footsteps paced in the shop below. The unlocked doors had presumably aroused some suspicion.

Augusta huddled beneath the desk with her arms around her knees and her back resting against the desk panel. There was just enough space for Fred to squeeze in next to her. All she could hear now was the sound of their breathing and the footsteps downstairs.

But now they were climbing upstairs. Each step seemed to thud with Augusta's heartbeat.

'They're coming in here, aren't they?' she whispered.

'This could be it,' said Fred. 'They might find us.'

They heard the door open, and the light switched on. Augusta closed her eyes against the sudden brightness.

Someone marched across the floor to the desk. Two shiny shoes and pinstriped trouser legs came into view.

They could only belong to Mr Fairburn. Augusta held her breath as he sat in his chair. Then he shunted it under the desk, bringing his knees just inches from Augusta and Fred.

The absurdity of the situation brought on an irresistible urge to giggle. But Augusta reminded herself of the humiliation she would suffer if he discovered them here.

Mr Fairburn tutted, then Augusta heard the dial of the telephone being turned. 'Clerkenwell 4756 please,' he barked at the operator. A moment later, he was admonishing someone. 'I've just returned to the shop to pick up some ledgers, and Barnabus has left everything unlocked! When I say everything, not quite *everything*. Fortunately, the shop door is locked. But the rear door, storeroom door, staircase door and the door to my office weren't locked at all! It's a disgrace! Ensure you have a word with the boy in the morning, won't you? We can't employ someone who doesn't do his job properly. Let him know I won't stand for it, won't you?'

The phone receiver was slammed back into position and silence fell.

Augusta breathed slowly and carefully through her mouth, wary of making the slightest noise. Fred clasped his knees and rested his forehead on top of them.

'What an absolute shambles,' muttered Mr Fairburn.

To Augusta's relief, he got to his feet and left his desk. He marched across the floor and a cupboard door was slammed, followed by some tutting. Then the light was turned off and the door was closed and locked. Augusta felt her body relax. She hoped it wasn't too soon to feel relief.

'Oh good grief,' whispered Fred. 'I thought I was going to faint with fear.'

'Me too,' said Augusta, listening to the reassuring

sound of Mr Fairburn's footsteps descending the stairs. 'I feel sorry for poor Barnabus in the morning.'

'Me too. It's all our fault he's in trouble.'

They waited a little while longer until the shop seemed to be in silence again.

'How do we know for sure that he's gone?' said Augusta.

'I suppose we don't. I can only assume he's got what he came for. I forgot he lives close by.'

'Close by?' Augusta hadn't realised this. 'Where?'

'Bloomsbury Square, I think.'

'That's very close by. He could come back any moment he chooses! I wish I'd known that before we came here.'

They uncurled themselves and crawled out from under the desk.

Augusta turned on her torch and had one last look among the papers, hoping to find something incriminating. A receipt from Mitchell's Great Hardware Store caught her eye.

'Look at this,' she whispered to Fred. 'Someone purchased a pot of red signwriter's paint two days ago.'

'Really?' He peered at it over her shoulder. 'We have evidence!'

'He would say the purchase of red paint isn't evidence he threw it over the shop. But we know it's him, don't we?'

Augusta nodded. 'In my mind, this confirms it. And instead of throwing away the receipt, Fairburn appears to have kept it so he can add it to his expenditure.' She laughed. 'It's just as well he's meticulous about his record keeping. We've caught him out! Let's leave now.'

Fred unlocked the door, and they tiptoed out.

'Shall we leave it unlocked again as a joke?' said Fred. 'He'll be angry at Barnabus and then wonder why he didn't lock the door himself.'

'Alright then,' said Augusta. 'Although how you can find the energy to be mischievous after that scare, I don't know.'

They crept down the stairs and into the dark shop.

Augusta had an idea. 'I won't be a moment, Fred.' She handed him her torch and went over to the bookshelves.

'What are you doing?' he whispered after her.

'I won't be long.'

She could just make out the neat displays of books. She went to one shelf, pulled out a book, then put it on another. Then she rearranged another. She transferred some more books to shelves on the opposite sides of the room and then mixed up a few more. As someone who liked books arranged properly by genre and author, she knew how much this would annoy Fairburn the following day.

Then she smiled to herself.

'What did you do?' Fred asked.

'Just rearranged a few things. It was extremely petty of me, but I couldn't help myself. Come on, let's get out of here.' She nudged his arm. 'And let's make sure we lock the outer door. Mischief is fine, but I wouldn't want Webster's to be robbed.'

Chapter 31

'HAVE you recovered from our secret mission last night?' Augusta asked Fred as they opened the shop the following day.

'I think so. I felt certain we were going to be caught when we hid under Fairburn's desk though! I can't say I'd like to repeat the experience.'

'Me neither. But at least we found some useful evidence.'

'Yes, we were successful on that front. Although I do feel a little sorry for Barnabus this morning.'

'Me too.'

The door opened and Philip stepped in and greeted them. He seemed a little happier than usual.

'This is a surprise,' said Augusta.

'It is, isn't it? And it's lovely and warm in here. I like the thought of making myself comfortable with a good book in one of these chairs.'

'You can!'

'No, I can't. The Flying Squad is keeping me busy.

That said, there's been quite a breakthrough which I had to come and tell you about, Augusta. I had a visit yesterday from Tommy Barnes.'

'He came to see you?'

'Yes, I was as surprised by it as you are. You'll never guess who he claims was behind the Hatton Garden robbery.'

'Who?'

'Sir Charles Granger.'

'The newspaper man?'

'Yes.'

'How does Tommy know this?'

'He was part of the gang who planned it, but he was kicked out and so his revenge has been to tell all.'

'And you believe him?'

'I think so. We'll soon be able to verify his story once we've rounded up all the people he's named. We've got men out there arresting them as we speak. They'll all be interviewed at different police stations so none of them have an opportunity to collude. We'll see what they say and find out whether they're brave enough to mention Sir Charles's name.'

'That's wonderful! So after having been at the Flying Squad for only two days, you've solved the crime!'

'I didn't solve it really. It was just luck that Tommy decided to speak to me. And it's not all resolved just yet. I must admit, I'm still surprised about Sir Charles. We'll have to do a lot more work before we can be sure he was definitely behind it.'

'I'm not surprised about it, I don't like him.'

'Apart from when he spent lots of money in your shop.'

'That was Sir Charles?' said Fred. 'He seemed nice.'

'Well, he isn't,' said Augusta.

'Interestingly, I read in *The Times* this morning that the editor of the *Morning Express* has unexpectedly resigned,' said Philip.

'Really?'

'With immediate effect, apparently. That's quite unusual, wouldn't you say? I'm no expert on the news-paper industry, but I think editors usually step down once a replacement has been found. His sudden departure suggests they must have fallen out. I would like to ask Sir Charles about it, but for the meantime, I'll keep away while we gather the evidence against him.'

'And you also need to get him to explain the dinner with Celia Hawkins.'

'I do. That was something else Tommy Barnes helped with. Apparently, Sir Charles told him he met with Celia because she wanted Tommy to leave the gang. She was appealing to Sir Charles to let him go.'

'That's the reason he dined with Celia?'

'That's the reason he gave Tommy. If it's true, then it means Celia knew about Sir Charles's double life. Did Sir Charles murder her to silence her about his criminal activi-ties? Was he even having an affair with her? Only Sir Charles can tell us.'

'But when he realises all the gang members have been arrested, isn't there a risk he'll run away somewhere?'

'Yes, there is a risk and the Flying Squad have got him under surveillance. They're particularly good at that. If he makes a move to run away, then they'll stop him.'

'So the net is closing in on Sir Charles,' said Augusta. 'I'm sure you'll find the evidence you need which proves he was in charge of the gang who robbed the jewellers. But murder is a much more serious crime and it wouldn't surprise me if he's done more to cover his tracks.'

'Possibly. But I think Sir Charles has been quite careless. For example, you'd think a man in his position would have used an intermediary to communicate with the gang. Ideally, they wouldn't have known who he was at all. And if he is responsible for Celia Hawkins's murder, it may not take us too long to find the evidence. Detective Inspector Petty is looking at the man with renewed interest now.'

At lunchtime, Augusta called in at the newsagents on Marchmont Street. 'Have you got any old copies of the *Morning Express* and the *Evening Gazette*?'

'They're all out the back bundled up and waiting to be returned to the printers,' replied the newsagent, peering at her through half-moon spectacles.

'Can I look through them, please? I would like a copy of each for the days you have available.'

'I've only got the past week.'

'That will do for now.'

'For older copies, you'll need to visit a library.'

He showed her to the stockroom and left her to untie the bundles. 'Make sure you tie them back up properly again,' he instructed.

That evening, Augusta laid out the newspapers on her dining table.

'If Sir Charles is involved in the robbery and the Tower Bridge murder, then it's going to be interesting to see how his newspapers reported on the incidents,' she said to Sparky.

She looked at a copy of the *Morning Express*, which had a large headline about the robbery on its front page. 'I can't imagine Sir Charles being happy about this,' she said. 'I wonder if that's why the editor left?'

The other editions of the *Morning Express* included articles about the Tower Bridge murder. When Augusta leafed through the editions of the *Evening Gazette*, she found little on the robbery or the murder.

'The *Evening Gazette* only devotes a few words to each of the incidents. Do you know what I think, Sparky? I think he spoke with his editors and one of them did as he was told and the other one didn't.'

She telephoned Philip and told him this.

'It certainly makes sense that Sir Charles didn't want his newspapers reporting too widely on his crimes,' he said. 'It's probably worth speaking to the editor of the *Morning Express* to find out his reason for resigning. I'll make a note of that now and get someone to speak to him.'

'I'd like to speak to Tommy Barnes again,' said Augusta.

'Why?'

'I spoke to Celia's friend Molly, and she told me a few things I'd like to discuss with him. And didn't you mention that Detective Inspector Petty spoke with some women from the gang in Bermondsey?'

'Yes, he did. I don't think he got anywhere with them, but that's not a surprise.'

'I'd like to speak to them.'

'Careful now, Augusta. They're criminals. I don't think you need to be speaking to Tommy Barnes or them. All these people are nothing but trouble. They can be unpredictable and dangerous too.'

'But if Petty got nowhere with the women in Bermondsey, perhaps I can? They might be more likely to speak to a lady. And a lady who isn't a policewoman.'

'That's a possibility.'

'So I need to try.'

She heard Philip sigh. 'Very well. I'll give you the addresses, they're written in my notebook. But mind how you go, Augusta.'

'Don't worry, I know how to get away at the first sign of trouble.'

Chapter 32

Mrs Saunders asked to speak to Mary in the storeroom. Mary's heart sank. Lucy had presumably reported to the manager that Mary had threatened her, and now she was going to be dismissed.

'Lucy gave me some money this morning,' said Mrs Saunders. 'It was the ten shillings she'd taken from the till. I owe you an apology, Mary, I'm sorry. She confessed she did it to get you into trouble. I didn't believe Lucy would be capable of such a thing, but it seems she's found your arrival here difficult. I didn't realise things weren't friendly between the pair of you. Why didn't you say something?'

'I didn't want to upset things by mentioning it.'

'I can understand that, I suppose. I'm sorry I accused you, it was wrong of me. I made an assumption, and it was unfair of me. I don't know what made Lucy suddenly decide to tell me what she'd done. I suppose her conscience got the better of her. I'll make sure you receive your full wages for this week. And I have to admit that I told my sister what I thought you'd done as well.'

'I know. She confronted me about it.'

'Oh no, she didn't, did she? I shall telephone her and correct her. What a difficult time you must have been having, Mary. Everyone thought you were a thief, and you were only trying to do your best. I shall ensure Lucy's punished.'

'There's no need for that. She's already realised the error of her ways and I'm sure she won't do it again. Thank you for the apology, Mrs Saunders, and I'm pleased you have the money back now. I think it's best we all forget about it. I enjoy working here and I'd like to do my best to get on with Lucy.'

'Good.' Mrs Saunders smiled. 'I've told her to make more effort with you and I'm sure you girls will see eye-to-eye very soon.'

Chapter 33

FALCON GROVE in Battersea was a street of scruffy terraced houses. Augusta listened to the rumble of trains on the nearby railway lines as she waited for Tommy Barnes to open the door.

Eventually he appeared, arms folded and a cigarette in his mouth. Despite the cold, he was shirtless and wore a vest tucked into his trousers.

'Oh, it's you,' he said. 'You're friends with the detective. Come in.'

Instinct told her not to. 'I'm fine here, thank you,' she said.

'Suit yourself.'

'Do you have a few minutes to talk?'

'Yeah.'

'Do you want to put something warmer on?'

'I'm fine. I don't feel the cold.' He leant against the doorpost and blew out a plume of smoke.

'I met with Celia's friend Molly the other day. She told me Celia was in trouble at work.'

'What sort of trouble?'

'You didn't know about it?'

'No.'

'Apparently, she stole some scarves and dresses.'

He rolled his eyes and shook his head. 'And to think she was always complaining about me.'

'She and Molly fell out over it so, at the time of her death, they weren't close friends anymore.'

'Why are you telling me this?'

'I thought you should know, because you might not otherwise find out.'

The real reason Augusta was here was because she wanted to decide for herself if Tommy had murdered Celia. She had learned he was a violent bully. Was he also a murderer? With the attention now on Sir Charles, there was a risk Tommy would be forgotten about. She had found him fairly honest when she had met him with Philip, but this morning his narrow eyes seemed a little steelier and she certainly didn't feel comfortable enough to step into his house with him.

'Are you quite sure Celia told you she was seeing Molly after work on the day she died?'

'Yeah. And I remember it because it was the second time in a week.'

'That was unusual?'

'Yeah.'

'So she had already told you she was meeting Molly a few days before?'

'Yeah.'

'And do you know if she did?'

'She said she did. She went out, and she was back by nine, which was the time I told her.'

Augusta doubted Celia had been meeting Molly on this occasion because she had learned the pair had fallen out. So where had Celia gone?

'Did you believe her?' she asked.

'I had no reason not to.'

'Did she tell you anything about the evening? Where they went?'

'I just assumed it was Molly's house. Thinking about it now, it could have been another lie. Who knows where she went? She's not here to ask anymore.'

'You must miss her a lot.'

'I do. This is all I've got of her now.' He stepped away from the door and returned with a framed photograph. It showed a young woman with fair wavy hair standing beneath a blossoming tree in a garden. It was sunny, and Celia was laughing.

'It's a lovely photograph,' said Augusta.

'It was taken in my ma's garden last year. And there's this one.' He fetched the studio photograph which Augusta had seen published in the newspaper. 'It don't look so much like her in this one, she's too formal in it. But it's all I've got now.' He shrugged and gave a sniff. 'I don't know what she was doing on the bridge that night, but I can tell you who probably does know.'

'Who?'

'Sir Charles Granger. You've heard of him?'

'I have.'

'He's taken everything away from me, that man. And I mean *everything*.'

Augusta caught a bus on Lavender Hill which would take her to Bermondsey. She estimated she had enough time to make the journey before getting back to the shop in time for Lady Hereford's weekly visit. As she watched the rainy streets of Battersea pass by the window, she tried to make up her mind about Tommy Barnes. When he had showed her the photographs of Celia, she had felt sorry for him. But was that how he had wanted her to feel? Could he really be a manipulative killer?

She got off the bus on Tooley Street and looked for Vine Street Buildings. Philip had told her they were a group of tenement buildings close to the riverside warehouses.

She found them at the end of a dismal lane: featureless blocks six storeys high which overlooked cobbled yards. She passed grubby-faced children playing in the rain as she looked for the flat belonging to Dora Jones.

She eventually found Dora's flat on the fourth floor. Dora was a thin-faced woman who looked no older than eighteen. She wore a tightly wrapped shawl, and a young baby was nuzzled against her chest. She stood on her doorstep and gave Augusta a stony stare.

'My name's Augusta Peel and I'm an investigator.'

'Investigator?'

'A detective. A lady detective, in fact.' She smiled, attempting to put the young woman at ease. 'I'm trying to find out what happened to Celia Hawkins, the lady who was murdered on Tower Bridge a few weeks ago.'

'I know who you mean. But I don't know anything about her.'

'I realise that. But I'd like to find out why Celia was visiting Bermondsey on the night of her death. I believe it could have something to do with the fact she was robbed on Tower Bridge about a month before her murder.'

'I didn't rob her!'

'I'm sure you didn't.' This was going to be difficult, but Augusta persevered. 'I'm not accusing you of anything at all, Dora, I'm just after information. I've heard you have friends who may be in a gang.'

'No! Who told you that?'

'I have a friend who's a police detective. But I'm not

working for the police, I'm just trying to help with the investigation because little progress has been made. I can see that life is difficult for you here and I appreciate you and your friends have to make money however you can. I'm not here to pass judgement on that or accuse you of anything. I'm just looking for help in catching the murderer. I'm sure you must agree it was an awful thing to happen so close to where you live.'

Dora nodded. 'None of the girls would ever murder no one.'

'I realise that. Do you mind if I come in and we can talk some more? Your baby must be getting very cold while I keep you out here on your doorstep.'

Dora nodded again. 'It's not much warmer inside.'

She let her into a sorrowful-looking room with a chair and a bed. There were a few coals on the fire, but it was unlit.

'How long have you lived here?' she asked, perching herself on the end of the bed.

'I've lived in this flat for a year, but I was born in these buildings.'

'You have family nearby?'

'Yeah, my ma and brother and sisters.'

'And how old is your baby?'

'Two months.'

'He seems very peaceful.'

'He is at the moment, but he soon lets me know when he needs something.' She gave a thin smile.

'Perhaps you or your friends saw Celia Hawkins here in Bermondsey before she died?' said Augusta. 'I'm puzzled by the fact she told no one she would be here. In fact, she lied about where she was going. It's frustrating me that I can't find an answer. You must know a lot of people here, do you have any ideas?'

The girl shrugged. 'None. But I can tell you that none of the girls would've murdered her. One of them might've robbed her that first time. Like you say, it's how we feed ourselves and our children. None of us are proud of what we do. Sometimes we get desperate. And when you see a lady who's got nice clothes and is carrying a bag, it's an easy thing to do.'

'Apparently, Celia's mother's wedding ring was taken when she was robbed. She was upset about it because her mother had died, and it had a lot of sentimental value.'

'That's sad. Most of the time, the girls just want money. And things which they can sell to get money. I don't know who robbed her that night, but if they'd known the ring was important to her then I don't think they'd have taken it. It would've been quick, and they'd have run off and left her unharmed. I'm not making excuses, I know it's bad and none of us want to do that sort of thing. I feel sorry for Celia.'

'I'm wondering if she came back to Bermondsey to find the ring,' said Augusta. 'Do you recall hearing about her doing that?'

'No, I never heard anything about that. I don't think I can help you, Mrs Peel. I feel sorry for Celia and I understand you're trying to do a good thing. But I'm no help. All I'm thinking about now is my baby boy and making sure he's got what he needs. I haven't been thieving for a while. My brother's been giving me money. I don't ask where he gets it from, but it helps me at the moment.'

'Maybe your friends might be able to help me?'

'They might be able to. Or they might not. Then there's Lizzie.'

'Lizzie?'

'Lizzie Clarke. I don't know where she is. I haven't seen

her for a few weeks. I've even tried looking for her, but I can't find her.'

'When did you last see her?'

'The day of the murder.'

'And you've not seen her since?'

'No.'

'What time did you last see her?'

'About five or half-past five. Then she went out for the evening.'

'Do you know where?'

'Just round here. She was working and when I say working, I mean stealing.'

'So she could have been on the bridge when Celia Hawkins was murdered?'

'She could have been. She wouldn't have done anything like that though. She would never have murdered someone.'

'But you haven't seen her since the murder?'

'No. I went to see her family, but her ma and sister haven't seen her. Then I spoke to Robbie, he was going steady with her for a while. But he hasn't seen her either. No one has.'

'Has she disappeared before?'

'No, never. I've known her for three or four years and she's never done this sort of thing before. I'm really worried about her.'

The door opened, and a woman walked in. Although she looked older than Dora, her face seemed prematurely lined. Her cheeks were gaunt, and she wore a cloche hat and a long, dark coat which looked suspiciously new and expensive. She smelt of drink. 'Who are you?' she said to Augusta.

'Don't start on her, Annie, she's alright,' said Dora.

'I want to know who she is!'

'Augusta Peel, I'm an investigator.' She didn't like Annie's cold, hard gaze. 'And I'm just leaving.'

'What are you investigating?'

'The Tower Bridge murder.'

'You think Dora did it?'

'No. I'm just asking for help because the victim, Celia Hawkins, came to Bermondsey that night and I'm trying to find out why.'

'It's none of your business.'

'It probably isn't.' Augusta didn't want to disagree with her. She got to her feet and turned to Dora. 'Thank you for your help.'

'Good, you're leaving,' said Annie.

'Don't be rude,' said Dora.

'I don't like people who ask questions. I don't trust them.'

Augusta cautiously sidled past Annie to the door and left.

Chapter 34

As AUGUSTA MADE her way down the stairs, she checked her watch and saw it was later than she had thought. She needed to get back to the shop in time for Lady Hereford's visit. She would have to get across Tower Bridge, then catch the tube from Mark Lane station to King's Cross.

It was raining heavily as she stepped out of the building. She was just about to head towards Tooley Street when she caught sight of an alleyway between the warehouses. She felt sure it would lead to the lane which ran parallel to the river. It would be a good shortcut to the bridge.

As she made her way towards the alleyway, she heard a shout behind her. She turned and saw Annie.

'Come back here! I want a word with you!' Augusta stopped and watched her march across the rain-drenched yard towards her. Annie's face was twisted with aggression, no doubt exacerbated by drink.

Augusta wondered if it was wise to stand her ground. She assumed Annie only wanted a word with her, but there was a risk she could be violent too.

Augusta took a step back and realised her decision was well-timed when Annie lunged forward and swung a fist at her. Augusta ducked out of the way, then turned and ran towards the alleyway.

To her disappointment, it opened out into a dingy courtyard instead of the lane she had been expecting. For a horrible moment, she thought it was a dead end. But then she spotted another alleyway in the corner of the courtyard. With Annie running after her, she took off to the next alleyway, and it brought her out onto the lane.

She turned right and ran along the lane, twisting an ankle as she ran on the uneven cobbles. The warehouses rose high on either side of her and walkways crossed the street over her head.

She had once been good at running. It had been a necessity for her work during the war. But a few years had passed since then and it wasn't something she had practised recently. She could hear Annie shouting after her. She ran on, her lungs aching from the exertion. Her throat was dry as she sucked in the air she needed to keep going.

Annie's footsteps were gaining on her. The woman was younger and clearly had the speed and agility of a street thief. The drink wasn't slowing her down. Augusta hoped she could get onto Tower Bridge before Annie caught her. Hopefully the presence of other people would dissuade a physical attack.

But was there even anyone else about?

The lane was longer than she thought. In a gap between the warehouses, she caught sight of the bridge's towers in the rainy gloom. Ahead of her, she could see the tunnel which led beneath the bridge. She managed to find the strength to run faster and got to the tunnel. But how could she get onto the bridge?

Before Augusta could give it any more thought, there

was a sharp tug on her coat and she was pulled to the ground. The collar of her coat was tight against her neck as she tumbled onto the cobbles. As she tried to loosen her coat from her throat, she felt a sharp kick in her back. Another kick swiftly followed.

'Don't think about coming here again!' yelled Annie.

Augusta curled into a ball and covered her head with her arms. She had been trained for situations like this, but could she remember what she had been taught? Her first hope was that Annie would soon tire.

But the blows to her back kept coming, and each one knocked the breath from her. There was a danger she would soon become too weak to fight back.

Was this what had happened to Celia Hawkins?

Did Annie have a knife?

Icy fear lurched in Augusta's stomach, but she managed to keep herself under control. It was important to think with clarity and act decisively.

Annie was strong, but the drink would have affected her reactions. If Augusta could manage something swift and unpredictable, she hoped Annie would be caught off guard.

She rolled over so she could see Annie. In this position, she risked a kick in the face, so she had to be quick. Focusing on her assailant's foot as it swung towards her, she grabbed Annie's ankle. The sole of her boot scraped her cheek, but now Annie's strength had gone. Hopping around, Annie tried to wrench her foot free. But Augusta wouldn't let her.

'Get off!' screamed Annie, trying with all her might to free her foot.

Now was Augusta's chance.

She tensed herself, then swung her leg as far as she could, aiming it for Annie's other foot.

In a short moment, Annie's leg was taken from beneath her and she cried out as she crashed to the ground like a fallen tree.

Augusta jumped to her feet. She didn't want to be here a moment longer.

She left the tunnel and found a stone staircase on the right. She climbed it and found herself on the bridge. She didn't stop running until she reached the other side.

Chapter 35

HALF AN HOUR LATER, Augusta sat in a chair by the stove in her shop while Lady Hereford's nurse applied soothing ointment to the graze on her face. Every bone in her body ached, but luckily she didn't feel seriously hurt.

'I can't believe you're not going to report this to the police, Augusta,' said Lady Hereford.

'They have enough to be dealing with.'

'But this madwoman is going about attacking people.'

'She attacked me because she didn't like me asking her friend questions about Celia Hawkins's murder.'

'Maybe she is the murderer?'

'Possibly. I'll mention it to Detective Inspector Fisher.'

'She needs to be arrested. It's no way to behave at all. It makes you wonder what sort of upbringing she's had if she thinks that attacking defenceless ladies is a suitable pastime.'

Augusta winced a little at the word *defenceless*. Did she really look that harmless? She had been trained to deal with difficult incidents during the war and she had got herself out of some tricky situations. But she had been unprepared to deal with what had happened to her in Bermondsey. Perhaps she shouldn't have run away? Maybe she should have remained in the yard and confronted Annie, then she could have thrown some punches herself. Being pulled to the ground while running had immediately put her at a disadvantage.

'They need to go down there and arrest her,' continued Lady Hereford.

'That would make matters worse.'

'Why?'

'Because I need Dora and her friends to confide in me. If Annie is arrested, then they won't be on my side anymore.'

Lady Hereford laughed. 'You think that Annie woman is on your side? It's pointless trying to make friends with some people. I know you like to think you can do it, Augusta, and you do a good job of it most of the time. But when someone has got their mind set against you, there's very little you can do. And you need to be especially careful when dealing with someone of a violent disposition.'

Lady Hereford's nurse stepped back and surveyed the scrape on Augusta's face. 'It's as clean as I can get it now.'

'Thank you.'

Fred handed her a cup of tea.

'Thank you very much, Fred.' Augusta took a warming sip. 'I haven't told you about the paint attack, Lady Hereford.'

'Oh no, what now?'

Augusta told her about the red paint which had been thrown over the window. 'And we know for sure that it was Mr Fairburn of Webster's bookshop,' added Augusta. 'We found a recent receipt for a tin of paint on his premises.'

'Despicable!' said Lady Hereford. 'I can't quite believe I'm hearing this! How dare he!'

'I feel as though he's trying to force me out of here.'

'And I'll ensure that doesn't happen! Do you want me to speak to Sir Pritchard?'

'Yes, I think it would be helpful.'

'Where is his shop?'

'On Bury Place.'

'Well, I shall ensure that his business is well and truly buried.'

'No, there's no need for that, Lady Hereford.'

'But he's trying to ruin you!'

'And he won't succeed.'

'No, he won't! Bury Place, you say? It's possible Sir Pritchard is the landlord there, too. Or it could be part of the freehold owned by my friend Lord Harewood. Let me make some enquiries.'

'Thank you.'

'That's if he hasn't fallen from grace.'

'Why would he have fallen from grace?'

'Well, it's happened to that newspaper owner, Sir Charles Granger. He's been arrested for managing a criminal gang! And they even think he could be behind the Hatton Garden robbery. Can you believe it?'

'Detective Inspector Fisher mentioned it to me.'

'Oh I see, so you can believe it. Well, it's left me quite shocked. Only last year I sat next to him at a dinner hosted by the Mayor of the City of London. I didn't like him then and I make a point of never reading his newspapers. That said, even though you dislike someone, it doesn't mean you're expecting them to be a criminal. Fancy carrying on like that!'

'I'm pleased he's been arrested.'

'So am I. Did Detective Inspector Fisher have something to do with it, then?'

'I think so.'

'He hasn't wasted any time since his return, has he? What a marvellous gentleman.'

Augusta phoned Philip that evening.

'How did you get on with the nice ladies of Bermondsey?'

'Alright.'

'Something went wrong?'

'Nothing much. One of them didn't like me asking questions.'

'What did she do?'

'Knocked me over.'

'Oh dear. Are you alright?'

'I'm fine, just a bit bruised.'

'I suspect you're being rather modest about it, Augusta. Did she attack you?'

'Yes, but I'm fine.'

'If you give me her name and address, I'll have her arrested.'

'Thank you, Philip, but it won't help at the moment. I might lose Dora Jones's trust if I get her friend arrested.'

She heard him sigh. 'Very well. But I think the woman should be arrested. What's her name?'

'Annie.'

'I'll make a note of that.'

'Thank you. The point of this call is to let you know Dora told me about a friend of hers who's been missing since the night of Celia's murder. Her name is Lizzie Clarke. She swears Lizzie would never have harmed Celia, but she is wondering if Lizzie saw something that night and has either been harmed by the killer or has run away to escape them.'

'Or she could be the murderer.'

'That's what I'm wondering. Dora is convinced she'd never do such a thing, but it seems an odd coincidence. Dora told me she's spoken to Lizzie's family and friends and tried to find her, but she's got no idea where she is.'

'It's certainly an interesting coincidence. Perhaps Lizzie was involved in the events of that evening in some way.'

'I think the police need to be looking for her. She's potentially a murder suspect.'

'I agree. Although the Yard is quite fixed on the idea of Sir Charles having been responsible now. The evidence is quite compelling. Celia Hawkins knew his secret, and he employed Tommy Barnes to commit robberies. The man had a lot to lose and, indeed, he appears to have lost it now.'

'But Lizzie's disappearance can't be ignored.'

'I agree. I'll speak to Detective Inspector Petty about it and perhaps an appeal can be made to the public asking if anyone has seen her. As I'm not working on the case, it's the best I can do Augusta.'

'And I'm grateful for it, Philip. So… how are things?' As soon as the words left her mouth, they sounded awkward.

'Things?'

'Things with… what's been happening with your family. How are you getting on?'

'Oh, those things. Well, I refuse to speak to my wife.'

'Why?'

'Because I discovered she was having an affair with an old schoolfriend of mine.'

'Oh no, Philip, I'm so sorry!'

'Don't be sorry. What's happened can't be changed.'

'When you say you refuse to speak to her, has she visited you?'

'She telephoned me and I put the receiver down on her. I'm not interested in anything she has to say. There are no possible excuses. Even if I did allow her time to explain, she would only blame my job for being the reason.'

'That seems unreasonable.'

'I know. And it is. My wife is unreasonable. *Estranged* wife, I should say. Anyway, I've just noticed the time, and it's actually quite late, isn't it? Enjoy the rest of your evening, Augusta and make sure you get some rest.'

Chapter 36

'I WANT you to tell them what a load of nonsense this all is,' Sir Charles said to his lawyer, Mr Hillsdown. 'Can they honestly believe everything they're told by a little worm of a man who has never worked an honest day in his life?'

Mr Hillsdown gave an impassive nod. In all the years he had known his lawyer, Sir Charles had never seen him express anything other than indifference.

The door opened and two police detectives walked in. The red-haired one introduced himself as Detective Inspector Petty and the other was the one with the walking stick and the bookseller lady friend, Detective Inspector Fisher.

Sir Charles raised his chin and pursed his lips, determined to say as little as possible.

The two detectives made themselves comfortable on the chairs opposite him in the spartan room.

'My client would like to know how long he is going to be kept in custody,' said Mr Hillsdown.

'Well, that all depends,' said Detective Inspector Petty.

'On what?'

'On how well this interview goes.'

Sir Charles couldn't resist a sneer. He couldn't bear how police officers spoke. Why couldn't they ever give a straight answer? It was something they expected from everyone else, and yet they were completely slippery when questioned about something themselves, never wishing to give too much away. They spoke to men like Sir Charles as if they were superior and yet they weren't.

He sniffed and stared at them.

'Sir Charles,' began Detective Inspector Petty. 'Can you tell me what you know about Frank Harrison?'

'Never heard of the man.'

'Really? Because he's heard of you. In fact, he claims to have been working for you.'

'The man's clearly delusional.'

'What about Jim Fardon? Is he delusional too?'

'Probably.'

'So how do these men know about you when you've never heard of them before?'

'Because I'm Sir Charles Granger. Everyone's heard of me.'

'Not everyone.'

'The people who matter know who I am.'

'And who are the people who matter, Sir Charles?'

'Politicians, industrialists, bankers… those types. The people who actually make a difference in this world. Unlike…'

'Unlike whom, Sir Charles?'

'Time wasters.'

'Do I infer from that you consider we're wasting your time?'

'Yes, you are wasting my time. A gang of crooks has fooled you.'

'No, Sir Charles. They've fooled you.'

Why had everyone turned on him all of a sudden? What had he done wrong? He had been wrong to trust them.

'You do realise these men will say whatever they can just to save their own skin?' said Sir Charles. 'They've been up to no good and now they're trying to blame someone else.'

'So why do you think they're blaming you?' asked Detective Inspector Fisher.

Sir Charles decided he'd done enough talking. He wasn't paying his lawyer a small fortune to sit next to him with his mouth closed. 'Mr Hillsdown will respond to your questions now, Detective Inspector.'

'My client has no further comment at this stage,' said Mr Hillsdown.

'It was merely a question which followed on from the previous one,' said Detective Inspector Fisher. 'And Sir Charles answered that one readily enough. I'm just wondering why eight men who have been interviewed separately at different police stations would all say the same thing.'

'Because they've colluded,' snapped Sir Charles, unable to help himself.

'How? They didn't have time to. We arrested them at several different locations at the same time. I find it incredible that all of them could have given us the same story when they had no idea they were going to be arrested.'

Sir Charles had no answer. He glared at his lawyer, and Mr Hillsdown cleared his throat. 'My client will not comment on that,' he said.

'That's because he knows these eight men are telling the truth,' said Detective Inspector Fisher. 'How can he defend himself against it? The answer is, he can't. It's certainly going to be very interesting when this goes to court.'

'It will not go to court,' said Mr Hillsdown.

Detective Inspector Fisher laughed. 'In which case you and your client need to give us a very good reason why it won't. At the present time, we've got the word of eight men against one. If Sir Charles has a good defence, now's the time to hear it.'

Sir Charles glared at the detective and exhaled slowly. He was being backed into a corner and he hated it. 'Those eight men, Detective Inspector, are the lowest of the criminal class. Do you honestly expect a jury to believe their word against mine?'

'When there are eight of them, yes.'

'But they so clearly benefit from speaking against me!'

'How?'

'Their own crimes will be dismissed as a favour for coming clean.'

'Coming clean? So that means they are speaking the truth?'

Sir Charles cursed under his breath. 'I meant to say, pretending to come clean. Each and every one of those men is a manipulative liar who is trying to save his own skin.'

'You seem quite familiar with them for someone who claims to have never heard of them.'

Sir Charles cursed again. He didn't like the way this detective turned his own words around and used them against him. He sat back in his chair and glared at him. 'You're an impertinent chap,' he said.

'It's not advisable to speak to a Scotland Yard detective like that.'

Sir Charles leaned forward now and thumped his fist on the desk. 'Do you need reminding who you're talking to, Fisher? You do realise that a quick telephone call to one of my friends could get you immediately dismissed? This entire investigation would be dropped, and it would all look very embarrassing for the Yard indeed.'

'If you would like to use the telephone now to speak to one of your friends, then you have our permission,' said Detective Inspector Fisher.

Sir Charles clenched his teeth. He hadn't expected the stupid man to suggest the idea. Usually, when he spoke to people in this manner, they were scared. What was wrong with this police officer? He thought he could do and say exactly what he liked.

'We shall discuss the details of the Hatton Garden robbery shortly,' said Detective Inspector Fisher. 'But before we get onto that, I'd also like to make it clear that you're going to be questioned about the murder of Celia Hawkins.'

'Not again! You've already asked me about her. It's quite obvious to everyone that Tommy Barnes is responsible for her death. A violent, unpleasant man who's carried out an untold number of crimes in his time. He's been leading you on a merry dance.'

'All the same, Sir Charles, now that we have you here, we're going to discuss the murder and the robbery in great detail.'

'My client cannot be detained here for that long,' said Mr Hillsdown.

'Why not?'

'Because it's unreasonable. And he needs breaks.'

'Oh, there will be breaks,' said Detective Inspector Fisher. 'And he can use those breaks to telephone his important friends and get me dismissed. But until then, we'll get on with asking our questions.'

Chapter 37

'PLEASE CAN I have a look at your newspaper, Fred?' Augusta asked.

'Yes, of course.'

She walked over to the counter, wincing a little from the pain in her side.

'Are you alright?' Fred asked.

'Yes I'm fine.' She decided that ignoring the pain and stiffness from the previous day's attack would encourage it to go away.

Augusta leafed through the paper until she found the article she was looking for. 'Good, I'm so pleased they've published this. Hopefully, someone will have seen Lizzie Clarke.'

'Who's she?'

'A woman who's been missing since Celia Hawkins was murdered.'

'How mysterious.'

'She's a member of a street robbery gang in Bermondsey. It's important she's found because she may have witnessed the attack. Or she could have committed it.'

'She could be the murderer? I thought Sir Charles was the murderer?'

'It could be either of them.'

'How confusing. I'm glad I'm not a detective, I wouldn't have the first clue about any of it. So we've got to be on the lookout for Lizzie Clarke, have we? What does she look like?'

Augusta read from the article. "'Lizzie Clarke was last seen at Vine Street Buildings in Bermondsey at half-past five on Monday the tenth of January. A description of the woman is as follows: aged twenty-two, height five feet, four inches, slim build, brown eyes, fair hair. Anyone who has seen the woman is requested to contact the police at their earliest convenience."'

'It will be interesting to see if anyone comes forward.'

Chapter 38

MARY ATE her breakfast and listened as the landlady read extracts of the *Morning Express* to Rupert the foppish actor. 'The police have arrested the gang who robbed the jeweller's shop in Hatton Garden. That was quick, wasn't it? They must have been tipped off. Oh, and look at this. It seems we need to be on the lookout for someone called Lizzie Clarke,' she read out a description which Mary recognised. '"Anyone who has seen the woman is requested to contact the police at their earliest convenience,"' she added.

Mary felt her cheeks burn as if someone was watching her. She didn't dare look up in case she gave herself away. She carried on eating as if she had no cares in the world.

'Why are they looking for her?' said Rupert.

'I don't know.'

Mary's heart thudded so loudly, she felt sure the land-lady and Rupert could hear it from where they sat.

'So you need to look out for her, Rupert.'

'I'll keep my eyes peeled, Mrs Flynn.' He got to his feet

and pushed his chair beneath the table. 'Thank you for another lovely breakfast.'

'That's alright, you have a good day now. And good luck with your audition.'

Once he had left the room, only Mary and Mrs Flynn remained. Mary gulped down the rest of her tea and got up from the table.

Mrs Flynn regarded her. 'I don't suppose you've heard the name Lizzie Clarke, Mary?'

'No. Who is she?'

'Did you not hear me and Rupert discussing it just now? The police want to speak to her.'

'Why?'

'I don't know. But the funny thing is, the description of the young woman could almost be you.'

'Me?'

'Height five feet, four inches, slim build, brown eyes, fair hair. Twenty-two years old.'

'I suppose it sounds a bit like me.' She forced a smile, pretending to seem amused. 'There will be a few women in London who look like that.'

'There will, I grant you that. But you haven't told me very much about yourself at all. And that makes me wonder.'

'Wonder what?'

'If you're Lizzie Clarke.'

'I really don't know what you're talking about.'

'Don't you? Really?'

'No.' She looked at her watch. 'I really must leave for work.'

She side-stepped Mrs Flynn and made her way out of the dining room. She didn't like the landlady suspecting her like this. She returned to her room and began packing her suitcase. Once she had finished work for the day, she would find somewhere else to stay.

Chapter 39

PHILIP CALLED in at Augusta's shop shortly before closing time.

'I thought I'd let you know there's been quite a response to the appeal for Lizzie Clarke's whereabouts,' he said. 'I suspect several sightings won't be of Lizzie at all. But there's one which intrigues me. A lady who works in the cloakroom of Fenchurch Street station said a woman matching Lizzie's description collected a suitcase from her early in the morning of Tuesday the eleventh of January. It was the morning after Celia Hawkins's murder. Apparently, she remembers it because she was struck by how the woman was completely wet through, as if she'd been out in the rain all night. She said she looked cold and tired. The woman apparently changed into some dry clothes which were in her case and, later on that day, the cloakroom attendant found the wet clothes discarded in the bin in the cloakroom. She found the entire affair rather odd.'

'How intriguing. Does she know how long the suitcase had been there?'

'Her records show it was deposited at the railway station the previous evening, but she wasn't on duty then. It was her colleague who accepted the case.'

'And she thinks the woman was Lizzie?'

'She said she matched the description of her. And by depositing a suitcase with a change of clothes at the railway station, the woman had clearly been preparing for something.'

'Murder?'

'Possibly. Fenchurch Street station is just over half a mile from Tower Bridge.'

'But where is she now?'

'According to the cloakroom attendant, she asked where she could catch a bus to Bloomsbury.'

Augusta's heart leapt. 'She's in Bloomsbury?'

'Possibly, maybe Holborn.'

'That's still close by!'

'Yes. The attendant told her to take the number 25 bus which doesn't go to Bloomsbury, but she told her she could get off at High Holborn and walk from there.'

'So we know she got as far as High Holborn.'

'Yes. Perhaps we can find the bus conductor who was on that route that morning. She may have mentioned an address to him and asked for directions from High Holborn. I'll speak to E Division and see if they can spare some men to knock at the doors of lodging houses.'

'But there are lots of those in this area!'

'I know. It could be a painstaking task.'

'And you're not even supposed to be working on the case.'

'You're right. But Detective Inspector Petty is busy with Sir Charles at the moment. Although he's interested in the whereabouts of Lizzie Clarke, I think he's more convinced that Sir Charles is his man and he's concentrating on getting him charged. It will certainly be good for his career.'

'Even though you told him about Sir Charles. You should be taking the credit, Philip!'

'I don't need credit. I just want to catch Celia Hawkins's murderer.'

'You don't think it's Sir Charles?'

'It could be Tommy Barnes. Sir Charles insists it's him.'

'He would, anything to deflect attention from himself.'

'And it could be Lizzie Clarke. If it wasn't for your chat with Dora Jones, then we would never have known she was missing.'

'But not for much longer. It sounds like we can find her!'

'I hope so, Augusta. We're relying on what a cloakroom attendant is telling us, so I'm praying that she's reliable and not sending us on a wild goose chase.' He checked his watch. 'I should get going, I have to get back to Willesden. My estranged wife is visiting with her mother and my son.'

'Oh.'

'I believe they want to collect some things to take back to Bognor Regis. I think Audrey wants to speak to me about something too, not that I'm interested. But I'll listen for the sake of Michael.'

'Well, it will be nice for you to see him.'

'Yes, it will.' He nodded. 'I'm looking forward to that. I don't know what Audrey has told him about me. I hope she hasn't said anything bad.'

'She shouldn't! Because you have done nothing wrong.'

'Nothing other than spend too much time at work according to her. Anyway, I hope that's not the reason which has been given because I don't want him to think bad things about me.'

'And I'm sure he won't.'

'Well, we'll see. He's still at an age where he believes everything he's told. That's the delightfully innocent nature of children, isn't it?'

Chapter 40

Tommy puffed on his cigarette and watched the cloud of smoke rise into the cold, morning air. Thirty yards away was the door of Brixton prison. Any moment now, Billy Goldman would walk out of there. The only person he could trust.

Tommy hadn't stopped smiling since he had heard about the arrest of the gang members and Sir Charles. How the mighty had fallen! Hopefully, they had all learned they couldn't treat him however they liked.

Now it was just him and Billy. They would have to be careful about what they did next. Tommy planned to suggest to his friend that they get out of London. He had a cousin in Birmingham who could help them get settled there. London held nothing more for him now.

The door opened and Tommy felt a grin on his face as his old friend stepped out and strolled towards him, carrying his few belongings in a sack. He looked a little stockier than before, the regular prison meals had clearly been good for him.

'Billy. Welcome to the outside world again.' Tommy

slapped him on the shoulder and handed him a packet of cigarettes. 'You're a free man now.'

But Billy only gave a half-smile. He lit a cigarette and inhaled on it.

'There's even some sunshine for you this morning,' said Tommy, attempting to lighten the mood. 'Well, it was out earlier, it's behind the clouds again. Hopefully, it will come out again later.' He listened to his words faltering.

Billy puffed out a large cloud of smoke. 'What's this I hear about you, Tommy?'

'What?'

'You talking to the coppers about everyone.'

'When?'

'I'm not stupid, Tommy. I heard all about it while I was inside. News travels.'

'They threw me out. They betrayed us.'

'Us? No one betrayed me, Tommy. I don't think they betrayed you either, they was just being cautious after what happened with Celia.'

'I didn't do it!'

'I'm not saying you did. But I can see why they threw you out.'

'So you're taking their side?'

'I'm not taking any sides, Tommy. And that includes yours.'

His shoulders slumped. 'But we have a future, Billy. With everyone else out of the way, we're free to do what we want!'

'You're right. But I've got issues with trusting you, Tommy.'

'You can trust me! How long have we known each other? Twenty-five years!'

'I don't think I can. And although I can't say I've got a lot of time for Sir Charles, you shouldn't have done that to him. He's powerful and he won't rest until he's got his revenge on you. It was a stupid thing to do, Tommy, a very stupid thing to do indeed.'

Tommy's stomach felt cold. Was it possible he hadn't thought things through properly? A sense of dread crept over him. He really was alone now. He had assumed Billy would be with him, but he wasn't. He wanted nothing more to do with him.

'I'll always be loyal to you, Billy.' His words sounded weak.

Billy looked over to the road where a motor car was pulling up. 'Looks like your friends have arrived, Tommy.'

He turned to see it was a police car.

'They're not here for me.'

'No? Well, they're not here for me either. I've got a clean sheet because I've only just stepped out of prison.'

Tommy recognised the red-haired detective who had interviewed him. He was accompanied by a constable.

'Mr Barnes,' said Detective Inspector Petty, as they drew close. 'Come with us please, you're under arrest.'

'What for?'

'For the murder of Celia Hawkins.'

'Again?'

'We have new information, Mr Barnes.'

The constable told him to put his hands behind his back and clipped on a pair of handcuffs. He tried not to wince as they pinched his wrists.

'Come and have a chat with us at the station, Mr Barnes.'

'But I had nothing to do with it!' he cried out as the constable led him towards the car.

He glanced back at Billy, but his old friend had turned away.

Chapter 41

SOMEONE HAD ATTEMPTED to repair *Tess of the D'Urbervilles* and done a terrible job of it. The book wouldn't close properly and pages had been glued into the wrong places. Augusta sighed, wondering whether it was worth her while trying to repair it. 'It's not exactly the cheeriest of reads,' she said to herself.

Fred knocked at the door and stepped in. 'Who are you talking to?' he asked.

'Myself. I was reminding myself that *Tess of the D'Urbervilles* isn't a happy story.'

'Are any of Thomas Hardy's books happy stories?'

'I can't think of any… there may be one.'

'It doesn't matter though, they're still excellent books.'

'Yes, they are. If you're in the mood for them.'

'Are you in the mood for Mr Fairburn?'

'Certainly not!'

'He's here to see you now.'

'What about?'

'I don't know. But he seems less… argumentative.'

'Really?' Intrigued, Augusta followed Fred into the shop.

Mr Fairburn cleared his throat when he saw her. 'Good morning, Mrs Peel.'

'Is it still morning?' She checked her watch. 'It's just turned midday.' There was something about Mr Fairburn which made her petty-minded.

'Good afternoon, then,' he said.

'How can I help?'

He cleared his throat again. 'I've come to say that... I may have misjudged you, Mrs Peel. Having considered everything, I realise now my accusations were slightly unfounded.'

'Only slightly?'

'Completely then. You must understand that business has not been as strong as usual recently and I care so much about my shop and my staff that I do whatever I can to keep our trade thriving. In recent weeks, I've been guilty of having been... too enthusiastic about the success of my shop, and it's led me into territory which... well, let's just describe it as uncharacteristic behaviour. It's not the sort of conduct I recognise. I would like to reassure you I have spoken with the agent of this property and clarified my position with him.'

'It wasn't just the agent, was it, Mr Fairburn?'

'I don't think so, no.'

'We had children in here pulling books off the shelves which left my assistant Fred with an awful lot of tidying up to do.'

'I see.'

'Are you going to apologise for that?'

'Erm, yes.'

'And there was the paint. It took Fred over an hour to clean it all up.'

'I see.'

'Do you apologise for that also?'

'Indeed. It was all most unfortunate.'

'You speak as if it happened by itself, Mr Fairburn.'

'Do I?'

'Yes. Do you actually take responsibility for the three incidents which were an attempt to intimidate me and Fred in the hope I would close my business?'

'Do I take responsibility for my actions? Yes.'

'And you're actually going to apologise for them?'

'Yes.'

'I haven't heard the word "sorry" pass your lips yet, Mr Fairburn.'

'Oh.' He scratched the back of his neck. 'I am sorry for any inconvenience which was caused.'

Augusta already felt tired of the conversation, she didn't want her time wasted by him any longer. 'You must excuse me, Mr Fairburn, but I have some work to be getting on with.'

'Of course.' He continued to watch her, as if expecting her to express thanks for his apology.

She turned away from him and spoke to Fred. 'Would you like to have a look at the copy of *Tess of the D'Urbervilles* and tell me if you think it's worth repairing?'

'Of course, Mrs Peel.'

As they went into the workshop, Augusta heard Mr Fairburn leave.

A more welcome visitor arrived later that afternoon. It was Philip. He bustled into the shop as enthusiastically as he could with a walking stick.

'Augusta!' he puffed. 'E Division has made a break-through.'

'Really?'

'They called at a lodging house on Southampton Row today and the landlady says one of her guests fits the description of Lizzie Clarke. She says this young woman is called Mary Willis but has told her very little about herself. The landlady has suspected for a while she might be hiding something. Apparently, she works for the landlady's sister at Saunders Animal Supplies shop.'

'Not the one on Grenville Street?'

'I think so.'

'But that's where I buy Sparky's bird seed from! Do you think this Mary could be the same woman the cloakroom attendant mentioned?'

'Could be. Southampton Row is a short walk from High Holborn where the woman who picked up the suitcase would have got off the bus.'

'This is good news.'

'It is, but there's a slight problem. The landlady has already confronted Mary Willis because she fits the description of Lizzie Clarke. The landlady is worried now that she's frightened her off. Apparently, she's already packed her things into a suitcase and the landlady is concerned she's going to move on as soon as she's finished work for the day. So two constables from E Division are currently on their way over to the shop where they'll speak to her.'

'But even if she is Lizzie Clarke, surely she can just continue to deny it? She's been living under a pseudonym since the murder. How can they prove it's her?'

'They'll need someone who knows her. How about Dora Jones?'

'Yes, she'll be able to tell for sure.'

'Dora trusts you much more than Detective Inspector Petty and his men. Would you mind visiting her and asking her to accompany you to Hunter Street police station? I'll send a message to E Division to hold her there.'

Augusta wasn't keen to encounter Annie again. Philip seemed to read her thoughts. 'How about I ask a couple of chaps from M Division to meet you there? Just in case there's any trouble from Annie again. I'll ask them to stay away from Miss Jones because we don't want her being frightened off by them. We need her help.'

'Alright then.'

'Thank you, Augusta. I don't know what I'd do without you.'

The compliment made her face heat up. She hoped he wouldn't notice. 'Thank me when we've finally got to the bottom of this, Philip.'

Chapter 42

'WE'RE GETTING A TAXI?' Dora said to Augusta as a constable from M Division hailed one for them on Tooley Street. Augusta felt relieved she had persuaded the young woman to join her, and there was no sign of Annie, either.

'Yes, we'll travel by taxi. It's much more comfortable than the tube when you've got a baby to carry.'

'But I'm used to carrying my baby.'

'I realise that. But it's nice to travel in a little more comfort when the opportunity arises.'

The constable opened the door of the taxi and Augusta thanked him as they climbed in. Once the door was shut, they headed towards Tower Bridge. It was already getting dark, and a damp fog was settling over the river.

'Did Annie hurt you yesterday?' asked Dora. 'I heard her run after you.'

'She tried.'

'I'm so sorry. She was drunk.'

'Don't be sorry, it's not your fault. I'm fine and it's all forgotten about.'

At the end of the street, the taxi turned left and made its way over Tower Bridge.

'I can't believe I'm going to see Lizzie again,' said Dora. 'I've been so worried about her.'

'*If* it's Lizzie,' said Augusta. 'We're not completely sure yet, which is why we need your help. If it is her, don't feel too hurt if she isn't pleased to see you. She's been trying to live under a new identity, and she's been taken to a police station. It's not what she wanted, so she may not be in the best of moods.'

Dora acknowledged this with a nod and Augusta felt sad for her. She lived a miserable existence in a tenement with a young baby to look after by herself. Her friend had gone missing and had possibly committed a serious crime. She hoped the experience at the police station wouldn't be too difficult for Dora.

She looked out of the window as they passed over Tower Bridge. This was the place where it had all begun. She could only hope the mystery would be resolved soon. Was Lizzie Clarke a perpetrator or another victim? Was Sir Charles responsible? Or even Tommy Barnes?

She hoped they would discover the answers very soon.

They climbed out of the taxi outside Hunter Street police station, an austere Victorian building just a short walk from Augusta's flat on Marchmont Street. The baby had been peaceful during the taxi journey, presumably lulled by the movement of the car. But now he was growing restless. Dora said some soothing words and rocked him a little, but it did little to improve his mood.

Inside the station, Augusta explained who she was to the duty sergeant.

'Sergeant Durbridge has been expecting you,' he said. 'Come this way.'

They followed him along a corridor to a small room. Augusta held her breath with expectation as he knocked at the door. What sort of reception would they receive from Lizzie Clarke?

When the door opened, Augusta gestured for Dora to go in before her.

A young woman with fair, wavy hair and spectacles sat sullenly at the table next to a constable. The sergeant paced the room, clearly impatient with having had to wait for them.

Here was Lizzie Clarke, the young woman missing from Battersea who had called herself Mary Willis and found a job in an animal supplies shop. It was clear from Lizzie's expression she didn't want to be here. But Augusta was struck by something familiar about her. Was it possible she had come across her before?

Dora stood in front of the table and stared at Lizzie. Lizzie stared back. Neither of them was reacting in the manner Augusta had expected.

Dora turned to Augusta. 'This isn't Lizzie.'

Sergeant Durbridge stopped his pacing and stared at Dora. 'This woman *isn't* Lizzie Clarke?'

'No.'

'Told you I wasn't,' said the woman. 'I'm Mary Willis. Now can you let me go, please?'

'How do you know this isn't Lizzie Clarke?' the sergeant asked Dora.

'Because I know Lizzie. Her clothes are different and she doesn't wear spectacles.'

He turned back to Mary. 'Can you remove your spectacles please?'

Mary sighed and did so.

Dora turned to Augusta. 'It's definitely not Lizzie,' she said. 'But she does look a lot like her.'

Augusta scrutinised the face of the young woman. Where had she seen her face before? Then she remembered.

There was a knock at the door and Philip entered. 'Sorry I'm a little late,' he said. 'How are you getting on?'

'We're not,' said the sergeant. 'This isn't Lizzie Clarke. You've been wasting my men's time again.'

'Oh no,' said Philip. 'Who is it then?'

Augusta felt sure now that she knew. 'She's not Lizzie Clarke,' she said. 'But I think she might be Celia Hawkins.'

Chapter 43

DORA'S BABY began to cry and the young woman attempted to lull him.

'Celia Hawkins?' said Sergeant Durbridge over the noise. 'That's the same name as the young woman who was murdered on Tower Bridge.'

'That's right,' said Augusta. The woman she was looking at bore a strong resemblance to the woman in the photographs which Tommy Barnes had shown her. 'I think the woman who sadly lost her life that night wasn't Celia Hawkins, it was Lizzie Clarke.'

'No!' cried out Dora.

Augusta turned to her. 'I'm sorry, Dora. I'd like to think I'm wrong, but…'

'You're never usually wrong about these things, Augusta,' said Philip. 'Can a chair be fetched for Miss Jones, please? And some hot sugary tea. She needs to be looked after.'

The constable got up from his seat, took his chair over to Dora and helped her sit down. The baby continued to cry. 'I'll put the kettle on,' he said before leaving the room.

Sergeant Durbridge rubbed his brow. 'I don't understand,' he said. 'The Yard has had my men running around Bloomsbury looking for a woman who isn't here?'

'Yes,' said Philip. 'But your time hasn't been wasted.'

'Why not?'

'Because we've discovered that Celia Hawkins changed her identity,' said Augusta.

'Have you?' the sergeant asked Mary Willis. 'Are you really Celia Hawkins?'

She said nothing, presumably worried she would incriminate herself if she spoke. The constable returned with tea for Dora. 'Luckily a pot had just been made,' he said. The baby was still crying.

'Would you like me to hold your baby for you while you drink your tea?' Augusta asked Dora.

'Thank you.' Dora carefully handed the wiggling child to Augusta. 'Is Lizzie really dead?' she asked as Augusta took hold of the baby in her arms. The change of scene seemed to pacify him a little.

'I suspect she may be. I'm sorry, Dora.' The young woman pursed her lips and lowered her head. The baby's face creased up again and Augusta began gently rocking him as she walked back and forth.

'If I remember rightly,' said Sergeant Durbridge, 'the body of Celia Hawkins was pulled out of the river at Rotherhithe, three days after she was murdered on Tower Bridge. They knew it was her because there was something in her coat pocket, wasn't there?'

'A small diary,' said Philip.

'That's right. And because she matched the description of Celia Hawkins, although...' he glanced cautiously at Augusta and the other women. 'I won't go into detail here about the effects of prolonged submersion on the human body. It suffices to say that it was fairly apparent the woman found in the river was Celia Hawkins. Now Lizzie Clarke looks similar to her, you say?'

Dora nodded. 'She does.'

'I've no idea who Lizzie Clarke is!' responded Mary Willis.

'Neither do I,' said the sergeant. 'Now let me clear this up.' He turned to Augusta. 'You're telling us Mary Willis here is actually Celia Hawkins?'

'Yes.'

'Even though we thought Celia Hawkins was murdered on Tower Bridge. And this lady isn't Lizzie Clarke. Nor is she Mary Willis, as she claims.'

'No,' said Augusta. 'I think she's Celia Hawkins.'

'So Celia Hawkins isn't dead, after all?' asked the sergeant.

'No. And I think she murdered Lizzie Clarke on Tower Bridge.'

'Isn't Sir Charles being held for the murder?'

'He is,' said Philip. 'Among other things. But I agree with Augusta, Miss Hawkins must be the culprit.'

'Just let me go home!' Celia cried out. 'I've had enough! I don't know what any of you are talking about!'

Augusta turned to her, still rocking the baby. 'You wanted to get away from your life, didn't you? You'd got yourself into trouble in the shop you worked in, you'd fallen out with your friend Molly and you wanted to leave Tommy Barnes. The thought of making a new start in life must have been quite appealing. And was it Lizzie Clarke who robbed you on Tower Bridge that night? Was it she who stole your mother's wedding ring? You were upset about that. You concocted a plan to take revenge on her as well as make a new start for yourself. Am I right?'

Chapter 44

CELIA HAWKINS'S SHOULDERS SLUMPED, and she stared down at her hands. Augusta hoped she would give in and tell everyone the truth. The baby fretted in her arms. His little fists thrashed about. She tucked them into the shawl and tried to soothe him.

'I wanted to start again,' said Celia.

'Get your notebook out, Smith,' said the sergeant to the constable. 'You'll need to get this down.'

Celia looked up at Augusta. 'Have you ever got yourself into such a mess that you wish you could start your life all over again?'

Augusta nodded. 'I think many people have had that thought.'

'But they don't then murder someone,' said Philip.

'She stole from me!' said Celia.

'Can you please tell us everything that happened?' said Philip. 'Start at the very beginning and explain it all properly. I don't want any more confusion.'

'Life didn't turn out the way I planned it,' said Celia. 'I was living with Tommy and working in a clothes shop. I liked my job, but I felt angry I couldn't afford any of the clothes we sold. I felt jealous of the ladies who came in and bought them. I wanted to be like them. But I couldn't be, especially as I knew Tommy made his money from thieving. He kept telling me he had a new scheme to get rich, but nothing ever came of it. I wanted to get married and have children but I didn't want to marry a man who thieved for a living. I wanted him to change his ways, and I wanted us to be respectable.

'I tried leaving him once, but he found me again. I felt there was no getting away from him. I did my best to change him, but that didn't work.'

'Is that why you met with Sir Charles?' asked Augusta.

Her jaw dropped. 'How do you know that?'

'You were seen with him at L'Épicurien restaurant in Covent Garden.'

'Does Tommy know?'

'Yes.'

Celia dropped her head. 'I couldn't think of anything else to do to stop Tommy from what he was doing. Sir Charles wasn't interested in helping me, though.'

'That doesn't surprise me,' said Augusta. 'Tell us about the robbery on Tower Bridge last year.'

'I'd been to St John's church in Bermondsey because it was the anniversary of my ma's death. Eight years. It was where she'd got baptised and married. She would've wanted to be buried there too, but they took her out to Brookwood. Miles away. Anyway, Tommy had got himself arrested in the City for pick-pocketing people in pubs, so I was walking over Tower Bridge to get to Old Jewry police station.

'I didn't expect any trouble on the bridge. I was distracted by the view of the river. It was getting dark, and I remember looking at the lights reflecting in the water. I should have been paying attention, but I wasn't. I was passing by the first tower when Lizzie jumped out at me. She pulled at my bag, but I refused to let go. That's when she threatened me with the knife. She told me to give her my jewellery, too. I pleaded with her not to take the ring, but she wouldn't listen. The knife was so close to me it caught on my coat. I worried she would really hurt me if I resisted. So I let her take the bag and the ring. Then there was a moment which was so strange, I felt like I was dreaming.'

A pause followed and Augusta grew impatient. 'What happened?' she asked.

'When Lizzie had what she wanted, she took a step back. And some light caught her face. It felt weird because… it was almost like looking in a mirror.'

'Really?'

'I think she realised it too because we just stared at each other. Everything seemed to stop for a moment. Then she just turned and ran off towards Bermondsey.'

'You're saying Lizzie Clarke looked just like you?' asked Sergeant Durbridge.

Celia nodded.

'Would you agree?' he asked Dora.

'Yeah, they look like each other. I can see the difference, but that's only because Lizzie was my friend.' Then she turned to Celia with a snarl. 'And you killed her!'

'Alright,' said the sergeant. 'I know it's difficult keeping calm, but it's extremely important. We can't let emotions take over.' He addressed the constable. 'Perhaps there's a room where Miss Jones and her baby can wait?'

'No,' said Dora. 'I want to stay. I want to hear what she says next.'

'Then it's important to remain calm. Please continue, Miss Hawkins.'

'After the attack, I was angry and upset. When I got to Old Jewry police station, I told them about the robbery, but they told me to report it at the police station on Bermondsey Street. I couldn't face crossing that bridge again that evening. So I left it and reported it a few days later. But I never forgot that woman's face. Have you ever met anyone who looks like you? The same face and hair. The same age. They could almost be you, but they're not. I went back to Bermondsey a few times, hoping I could find her.'

'Why?' asked Augusta.

'Because I struggled to believe someone else could look so similar, as if she was my twin. And I had an idea that I could get my ma's ring back from her. So I went there and carried a knife of my own. Just in case she saw me and attacked me again. On my third visit, I saw her talking to a friend near the bridge and luckily she didn't notice me. As I watched her, a plan formed in my head. I was so fed up, you see. I wanted to change everything in my life, and I realised then how I could do it. If everyone believed I was dead, I could start all over again. Tommy wouldn't find me. I could pretend to be a different person and hopefully I'd meet a respectable man and get married.'

'And you decided murder was the answer?' said Philip.

Celia nodded. 'You don't know what it was like. I was desperate. And I needed money for my new life, so I began stealing from the shop. My friend Molly found out, and it ruined our friendship. She tried to help me and said she wouldn't report me if I repaid the money. But I couldn't, because I needed it. Then I took some dresses and sold those. Molly found out, and I knew I was going to lose my job. I was arguing with Tommy all the time and I realised the time had come. I had to go.

'So I went down to Bermondsey and I found Lizzie. I'd

worked out by then the places she liked to go. It was strange speaking to her again, but I told her I had money, and she was soon interested in what I had to say. I told her I wanted to buy the ring back, even though I knew there was probably no chance of it being found. She said she didn't know where the ring was, but she'd try to track down where it had got to. We arranged to meet again on Tower Bridge on the evening of the tenth of January.

'Once that was arranged, I knew I had to get on with my plan. I booked a week's stay at a lodging house on Southampton Row. Then I bought a second-hand suitcase, filled it with some clothes and money, and put it in the cloakroom at Fenchurch Street railway station. The suit-case was all I needed for my new life. Then I met Lizzie on the bridge as we planned.'

She bowed her head. The room was silent. Even the baby was settling down again as Augusta cradled him.

'We talked about the ring and the money,' said Celia. 'She couldn't find the ring but said she would keep trying. When she turned away from me at the end of the conver-sation… that's when I did it. I swapped our coats, and I left my diary in the pocket so people would assume she was me. I swapped our shoes too. Her feet were a little smaller than mine. Then I lifted her up and pushed her over the wall.' She sank her head into her hands. 'It was hard. So much harder than I thought it would be! And all the while, I felt sure someone would come along and see me. In fact, I was sure for several days afterwards that someone had seen something. I was shaking and trembling, horrified by what I'd done. I spent the night in a churchyard, but it was very cold, even though I was wearing her coat. The rain didn't stop.

'When I got to the cloakroom at Fenchurch Street station, the cloakroom attendant was looking at me because I was wet through. I got changed and, when I stepped out of that railway station, I was a new person. I was Mary. I decided to forget about my past completely and become a new person. And it worked. For a short while, anyway.'

'Poor Lizzie,' said Dora. 'I know she wasn't perfect, but she didn't deserve to die in that way. She was a good friend to me.'

'She was a thief,' said Celia.

'And so were you!' retorted Dora. 'What made you think you were any better than her?'

Celia had no answer.

'We'll take you home now, Miss Jones,' said Sergeant Durbridge. 'I'm sure you and your son have had enough for one day.'

Chapter 45

Philip walked with Augusta to her flat on Marchmont Street.

'I don't think we could have solved that without your help, Augusta,' he said. 'If you hadn't got Dora Jones talking, then we'd still be looking for the culprit in the Tower Bridge murder.'

'I'm sure you would have solved it, Philip.'

'I'm not sure I would have. I would still be trying to make my mind up between Tommy Barnes and Sir Charles Granger. At least Tommy can be released now without charge.'

'He was arrested again?'

'Sir Charles insisted he was responsible for Celia's murder and so Petty had him arrested a second time. Tommy Barnes insisted Sir Charles was responsible. They both pointed the finger at each other. But at least we have enough information now to charge Sir Charles with his criminal activities. Quite a fall from grace. As for Tommy... I suppose he'll go back to what he did before. It's difficult to imagine him changing his ways.'

'It's going to be quite a shock for Tommy when he discovers Celia Hawkins is still alive.'

'Yes, it is. He might want to visit her, mightn't he? I can't imagine how that conversation will go. It would be interesting to be there, wouldn't it?'

'I think I'd be happy to leave them to it. Are you going to stay with the Flying Squad for the time being?'

'Who knows? I was moved there to help with the Hatton Garden robbery and with that now solved too, perhaps I can put my feet up.' He turned to her, and she could just see his smile in the gloom. 'I'm joking, of course. There's always something to keep us busy. I shall wait and see what I'm assigned to next. I must say the structure and rules of the Metropolitan Police frustrate me a little. It would be nice to have some more freedom. That's why I envy you.'

'Envy me?' Augusta laughed. 'I'm just a middle-aged book repairer who sells cheap second-hand books.'

'You're much more than that, and you know it.'

His compliment embarrassed her, she didn't know how to reply. 'Thank you.' She felt the need to change the subject. 'How did yesterday go?'

'Yesterday?'

'When your wife visited.'

'Oh that. As well as it could have gone, I suppose. We've agreed my son is going to visit me once a month.'

'That's good news.'

'I would like it to be more often, but it will have to do for now. I've realised it's important for me to remain on good terms with my estranged wife, even though I can't forgive her for her behaviour. I have to be as considerate as I can for the sake of my son.'

They reached the door by the tailor's shop.

'Well here we are. Goodnight Augusta.'

'Goodnight Philip.'

'Until next time.'

'Don't disappear like that again, will you?'

'Why? Were you worried about me?'

'Yes I was! And I missed you. If you must go away then tell me first.'

'Alright then. I will.'

'Is that a promise?'

'Yes it's a promise.'

They exchanged a smile. Then Philip turned and she watched him walk away, leaning on his stick for support.

Chapter 46

'I THINK you need to explain it to me again, Augusta,' said Lady Hereford. She sat in her bath chair the following morning, feeding bird seed to Sparky. 'It wasn't Celia Hawkins who died, but someone who looked like her?'

'Yes. Celia Hawkins faked her own death.'

'By murdering someone who resembled her?'

'That's right.'

'What a thing to do! There are some very strange people about these days. How does one even come up with a plan to do something like that?'

'Someone with a twisted mind,' said Fred.

'Quite unbelievable.' She shook her head. 'I'm pleased Detective Inspector Fisher returned, Augusta, so you could help him solve it. How is he coping since his marriage ended?'

'I'm not sure. He doesn't talk about it a great deal.'

'Men don't like to talk about such things. You'll have to encourage him to do so.'

'Me?'

'Yes. Why not you? He holds you in high regard, I can tell.'

'You haven't seen him for some time.'

'I remember thinking it when I saw him last year. Now tell me, did Mr Fairburn pay you a visit?'

'Yes, he did. He called in yesterday to apologise.'

Lady Hereford laughed. 'Good! I spoke to Sir Pritchard and discovered he's also the landlord of several properties on Bury Place. He was quite horrified when I told him what Mr Fairburn had been up to. I shouldn't think you'll get any more trouble from him now.'

'I feel sorry for his staff,' said Fred.

'So do I,' agreed Lady Hereford. 'I wouldn't be surprised, Augusta, if you have some of them enquiring about jobs in here.'

'I don't need anyone else,' she said. 'I have Fred.'

'But can poor Fred manage on his own when you're gallivanting about with that dashing inspector?'

'Gallivanting?'

Lady Hereford laughed. 'I knew that description would irk you. You do much more than gallivanting, Augusta, I realise that. But seriously though, you should consider hiring someone to help Fred if your sleuthing begins to take up more of your time.'

'I doubt it will. It's only an occasional case here and there.'

'Nevertheless, it pays to think about it Augusta. You never quite know what you'll get involved in next.'

The End

Historic Note

The iconic Tower Bridge was built between 1886 and 1894 and is constructed of two towers linked by two walkways. The road part of the bridge is divided into two sections which are raised to allow large boats to pass beneath. The bridge opens about twice a day. In 1894, it opened, on average, seventeen times a day to allow access to the wharves and quays for central London's warehouses and factories. These heavy industries left central London during the 20th century and much of the boat traffic on this section of the river now is for pleasure.

The bridge's distinctive neo-Gothic style, featuring decorative turrets and intricate details, has made it a famous landmark. As mentioned in this story, the ornate stonework is cladding around a steel structure. The bridge would be fully functional without the cladding, but wouldn't look at all pretty!

The steel parts of the bridge were painted in a red, white and blue colour scheme to celebrate Queen Elizabeth II's silver jubilee in 1977. The bridge has had this colour scheme ever since. It is maintained - like all the bridges in central London - by the ancient Bridge House Estate which was established in 1282.

In 1952, a double decker bus had to jump the gap on the rising bridge when the bridge watchman forgot to ring the warning bell and close the gates. As the southern section of the bridge began to rise, bus driver Albert Gunter managed to get the bus and 20 passengers across the gap and onto the northern section, which hadn't yet begun to open. Albert suffered a broken leg, but his passengers were uninjured and the bus undamaged. Albert received an award of £10 and a day off work. I couldn't find out what happened to the watchman who forgot to do his job!

The tube stations close to the Tower of London and Tower Bridge have a confusing history! I'll do my best to explain it here.

Mark Lane tube station was built by the Metropolitan District Railway in 1884. It was constructed close to the Tower of London tube station, which was built by a rival company, the Metropolitan Railway, just two years previously. The Tower of London tube station subsequently closed when Mark Lane station opened. Mark Lane was then renamed as Tower Hill station in the 1940s.

However, with not enough room for expansion, Tower Hill station was closed in 1967 and a new one built on the location of the original Tower of London station. When you get the tube to the Tower of London today, you're on the site of the first station which was built in 1882. It has some of London's Roman wall incorporated into its structure and there is a section of the Roman wall visible outside Tower Hill station too.

Bermondsey, on the south bank of the River Thames, was an important manufacturing area of London until the early 20th century. Traditionally, the area was home to industry which was deemed too smelly or noisy to be carried out across the river in the City of London.

Leather, beer, gin, vinegar, biscuits, preserves, hats, glue, gunpowder and rubber were just some of the products processed in Bermondsey's factories and their chimneys constantly pumped smoke and malodorous smells into the south London air. Bermondsey was also home to some notorious slums which received a mention in Charles Dickens' Oliver Twist.

Vine Street Buildings, where Dora lives, was a collection of tenement buildings which were presumably built to provide low-cost housing for Bermondsey's workers. They no longer stand after this area was bombed during WWII. What remained was largely redeveloped between the 1960s and 1980s. The street where Annie chases Augusta has now gone and the warehouses have been replaced by green space, offices, hotels and restaurants.

Publishing began in Fleet Street in the 1500s and was soon joined by many legal and financial institutions. By the late 18th century, the street had become synonymous with the British newspaper industry. The Daily Courant, the first British daily newspaper, was published on Fleet Street in 1702. Over time, several prominent newspapers and publishing houses, including The Times, The Daily Telegraph, and Reuters, established their offices on Fleet Street. Many famous writers, including Charles Dickens, Samuel Johnson, and Mark Twain, worked in the area. In the late 20th century, technological advancements led to the relocation of many newspaper offices away from Fleet

Street. The last major newspaper, The Daily Telegraph, left in 1989.

Nowadays, just a few publishers remain in Fleet Street, but the many pubs and bars once frequented by journalists are still popular with city workers.

Thank you

Thank you for reading *The Tower Bridge Murder* I really hope you enjoyed it!

Would you like to know when I release new books? Here are some ways to stay updated:

- Like my Facebook page: facebook.com/emilyorganwriter
- Follow me on Goodreads: goodreads.com/emily_organ
- Follow me on BookBub: bookbub.com/authors/emily-organ
- View my other books here: emilyorgan.com or scan the code on the next page.

And if you have a moment, I would be very grateful if you would leave a quick review of *The Tower Bridge Murder* online. Honest reviews of my books help other readers discover them too!

Also by Emily Organ

Penny Green Series:

Limelight
The Rookery
The Maid's Secret
The Inventor
Curse of the Poppy
The Bermondsey Poisoner
An Unwelcome Guest
Death at the Workhouse
The Gang of St Bride's
Murder in Ratcliffe
The Egyptian Mystery
The Camden Spiritualist

Churchill & Pemberley Series:

Tragedy at Piddleton Hotel
Murder in Cold Mud
Puzzle in Poppleford Wood

Also by Emily Organ

Trouble in the Churchyard
Wheels of Peril
The Poisoned Peer
Fiasco at the Jam Factory
Disaster at the Christmas Dinner
Christmas Calamity at the Vicarage (novella)

Writing as Martha Bond

Lottie Sprigg Series:

Murder in Venice
Murder in Paris
Murder in Cairo
Murder in Monaco

Limelight

A Penny Green Mystery Book 1

How did an actress die twice?

Penny Green has lost her job. Once admired as Fleet Street's first lady reporter, she's been dismissed for criticising a police decision. So when Scotland Yard calls on her help in a murder case, she's reluctant to assist.

But the case perplexes her. How was a famous Victorian actress shot in Highgate Cemetery five years after she drowned in the River Thames? It makes no sense.

Penny's personal connection to the murdered actress draws her in. As does the charm of Scotland Yard inspector, James Blakely. But her return to work sparks the attentions of someone with evil intent. Who is so desperate to keep the past hidden?

Find out more here: mybook.to/penny-green-limelight

Tragedy at Piddleton Hotel

A Churchill & Pemberley Mystery Book 1

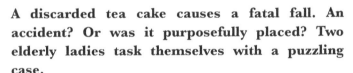

A discarded tea cake causes a fatal fall. An accident? Or was it purposefully placed? Two elderly ladies task themselves with a puzzling case.

When widowed Annabel Churchill leaves London and buys a detective agency in the village of Compton Poppleford, she's faced with a murder investigation. Teaming up with eccentric spinster, Doris Pemberley, she vows to crack it.

The death of local busybody, Mrs Furzgate, at the local hotel leaves the villagers vexed and the constabulary clueless. Churchill and Pemberley fuel themselves with cake and quiz a range of local characters. What's the connection with Mr Bodkin the baker? And why did Mrs Furzgate fall out with the Women's Compton Poppleford Bridge Club?

It's soon apparent that many people bore Mrs Furzgate a grudge. But when Inspector Mappin accuses the senior sleuths of meddling, they're in danger of never finding the killer…

Find out more here: mybook.to/tragedy-hotel